Cirena drew me forward with that delicate steel grip.

"What would you do? Waste your boon and wish me away?"

My boon for sparing her Anna. Not a chance in hell I was stepping into her twisted world by accepting her offer to dance.

Not a chance in hell.

"What do you want, Cirena?"

"You misunderstand me, young one. I've simply come to bring you a message: The one who sought to save your soul, the one who so foolishly, so very foolishly fought for you, he languishes in the prison of that hospital. Your beautiful Matteo, soon he will be forced to sacrifice yet another piece of his humanity to the Huntress. For serving as your protector...he...will...fall."

The last rush of her breath brushed across my cheek.

"Matteo?" I whispered.

But Cirena was already stepping backward into her shadows, gathering them around her, filament by filament until they shrouded all but her voice.

"Will you save him?"

Praise for
The Shades of Venice series
Episode One: Faces in the Water

"A little surreal, kind of like Alice falling down the rabbit hole or walking through the mirror; only this little Alyse has claws."
- *Mindy Wall*, **Books, Books, and More Books**

"This book kept me on the edge of my seat the whole way through. Tonya's characters were flawed and riveting. I enjoyed the bits of history about Venice and the fairytale like quality throughout the book. A dark fairytale, but one none the less. The ending had an unexpected plot twist that was a pleasant surprise. I cannot wait to read the next book."

- *Tracy Zuver*, **Tracylovesbooks**

"You don't need to have read dozens of books in the 80s strewn with words like 'wetware' and 'augmentations' to enjoy what is a soundly spooky tale of a strong female coping with, well, lots of bad stuff. ... Nice Venetian touches include having boats dock picturesquely at the balcony of the Doge's Palace and our heroine taking refuge on a boat inside the flooded church of San Giovanni Grisostomo, ruined with its campanile fallen through the roof. Like the best of this genre the book combines unsettling invention with grounding details and emotions. It ends not on a cliff-hanger, but still unresolved..."

- *Jeff Cotton*, **Fictional Cities: Venice, Florence, London**

"This book is solidly written with tense action and emotional drama that can only be described as heart pounding. Few writers can take you into a world so different than your own and make it so real you look up and expect to see the characters in your living room. Do yourself a favor and read this tantalizing treat from a new powerhouse writer, Tonya Macalino."

- *Andy R. Bunch*, **author of SUFFERING RANCOR**

Praise for
Spectre of Intention

Amazon Reader Reviews:

"'Spectre of Intention' is a cross-genre triumph. Tonya Macalino spins a story webbed with threads of romance, science fiction, mystery and thrill—all cocooned into one gripping ride."

"Both the read and the ride are fast, furiously addictive, and fantastically executed. Overall, a damn fine read!"

"If you like reading character-driven fiction with a strong protagonist and a deft narrative style that never interferes with an old-fashioned ripping good yarn, then Spectre of Intention should be your next read."

"Tonya Macalino – remember this name. You'll be seeing a lot of it in the years to come."

"The villains are bad, the heroes are good, and yet they all manage to rise above stereotypes and cardboard cutouts to become real people with real motivations that the reader can truly care about. All in all, a fabulous first novel, and one that I'm sure will build a fanbase eager for more of Macalino's work."

"I highly recommend it for anyone who likes their romance with a lot of mystery, history, sci fi and paranormal aspects all rolled into one!"

Media Reviews:

"Spectre of Intention had me from the beginning... I couldn't read it fast enough!!... I look forward to reading more from Tonya Macalino! I recommend this book to others and purchase it as a gift. Put it on your TBR list!!"

        - *Melissa Rheinlander*, **Keeping Up With The Rheinlanders**

"Spectre of Intention is a fantastic read . . . a novel that puts a very sci-fi spin on what initially seems to be a traditional caper, but quickly becomes something more....This is a very dark, very edgy, very creepy story, but there are some moments of romance and humour. It's a very tense read, and one that almost demands your full attention, so the brief mood changes are definitely welcome. Fast-paced, with well-written dialogue, and a mystery that teases you from chapter to chapter, this was definitely a fun read."

        - *Sally Bibrary*, **Bibrary Book Lust**

"The author skillfully winds us in future-tech woven with psi-abilities and explores every person's right to privacy. Action-packed, *Spectre of Intention* is ripe with physical vocabulary designed to keep you attuned to Kaitlin's fear and longing. An intelligent, well-researched scifi is always good to find, and I learned a ton about space elevators. The human story in this book balances the physical science for the technically impaired, mixed in with spicy scenes of passion between the heroine and Cam Glaswell (fans self)."

        - *Kelly McCrady*, **author of The Empire's Edge**

"Tonya Macalino is definitely a writer to watch! SPECTRE OF INTENTION is a fresh, intriguing novel with a captivating heroine."

        - *Donna Fletcher Crow*, **author of A Very Private Grave**

stand alone titles
from Tonya Macalino

Spectre of Intention

The Shades of Venice Series

Episode One:
Faces in the Water

Episode Two:
Stealing Lucifer's Dreams

don't miss
The Shades of Venice: Episode Three
Portrait in Veronese Green

coming Fall 2014.

THE SHADES OF VENICE: EPISODE TWO

Stealing Lucifer's Dreams

Tonya Macalino

CRYSTAL
MOSAIC
BOOKS

STEALING LUCIFER'S DREAMS

Text:
Copyright © 2014 by Tonya Macalino
Excerpt from PORTRAIT IN VERONESE GREEN Copyright © 2013 by Tonya Macalino

Cover:
Photograph Copyright © Shutterstock
Cover design Copyright © Lisa Holmes

Excerpts:
Excerpt from Venice: Tales Of The City by Michelle Lovric (Copyright © Michelle Lovric) Reprinted by permission of A.M. Heath & Co Ltd.
Excerpts from Veronica Franco: Poems and Selected Letters by Margaret F. Rosenthal and Ann Rosalind Jones (Copyright © Margaret F. Rosenthal and Ann Rosalind Jones) Reprinted by permission of University of Chicago Press.
Translation of Lines 40-48 of Veronica Franco's Capitolo 3 Copyright © 2013 Ann Rosalind Jones
Excerpt from Selected Poems by Octavio Paz translated by Muriel Rukeyser, published by Bloomington Indiana University Press © 1963.

For information, address Crystal Mosaic Books, PO Box 1276 Hillsboro, OR 97123

ISBN: 978-0-9836303-9-5

Printed in the United States of America

Author's Note

When you decide to become a parent, it is seldom that you comprehend the extremes to which your life will change. No one can prepare you for all of the surprises along the way and how dramatically your time will become consumed, at first by feedings and changings, then by preschool runs and doctor visits, and then by mismatched school schedules and activities.

A quick stay in the hospital drove home the realization that I could not do it all. Since we last came together to share a story around the bonfire, I closed Rustling Sage, my bath and body company, and scaled back my writing in order to give my focus to getting my last kid through kindergarten...and staying out of the hospital.

Two years later and we've come out the other side. The book in your hands only came to life through the support of some very special people:

My family: Ray, Damien, and Heléna who kept cheering me on with hugs and little words of encouragement and even drove me clear across town to a private studio just so I could focus for a while. I'm truly a lucky girl.

My neighbors: Dana and Brad Silvers, Marisol and Reed Levick, Lisa and John Ohnstead, Amy and Corey Weinheimer, Jay and Ginger Cox, Lynn and Jason Horihan, and Senaida Perez who pitched in with the kids, the dishes, and a sympathetic ear during the worst of the chaos. You all are heroes in my eyes!

My Tuesday Night Write In crew: Doug and Dawn Sellers, Maggie Rivera, Pam Bainbridge-Cowan, Brad and Leah Wheeler, Brad Cameron, and all the others who give me a writing "appointment," a chance to laugh, the freedom to be a word nerd, and a place where my name isn't Mommy.

My translators: Susan Keesling who looks over obscure Venetian poetry for no other reason than she's got a big, beautiful heart! And Professor Ann Rosalind Jones who graciously and generously took time out of her sabbatical to translate and to convert to rhyming form, lines 40-48 of Veronica Franco's Capitolo 3.

My marketing buddies: The Myth Makers literary group, which consists of authors Brad Cameron and Ray & Damien Macalino, bookstore owner Tina Jacobsen, and our publicist Cassie Crosby who all work daily to keep my chin up and my career moving forward!

My editors: Trixy and Jack Buttcane, Ray Macalino, Rob Richards, Tom Cutts, Margaret Hammitt-McDonald, Charlena Miller, and Teri Watanabe who give up huge tracks of their time to keep me from looking like an idiot!

My fact checker: Trixy Buttcane who spent hours mapping the labyrinth of Venetian and Montana history and folklore to make sure I hadn't misunderstood any of my sources. I fully expect she will haunt me in my nightmares for any artistic license I chose to retain!

My fellow NIWA members (www.niwawriters.com): Mike Chinakos, Adam Copeland, Pam Bainbridge-Cowan/P.J. Cowan, Brad & Leah Wheeler, Andy Bunch, Jennifer Wilis, William Hertling, Chad Coenson, Anna Brentwood, Courtney Pierce, Brad Cameron, and so many others who keep me fired up and challenge me to make my work its professional best.

Quote Credits

The majority of the quotes used in STEALING LUCIFER'S DREAMS are short enough to fall under fair use (though I have requested permission for all of them). Nonetheless, I firmly believe an author should receive credit for their work...and anytime I can send a fellow author a new reader, it always brings me joy.

Luciana's warning to Alyse, "To give oneself as prey to many" is taken from a letter by the great poet/courtesan Veronica Franco. This translation can be found in VENICE: TALES OF THE CITY, an anthology by Michelle Lovric by Abacus, an imprint of Time Warner Books Group UK © 2003.

Matteo's lament, "I live, if a person can live / when her soul is wandering, banned," is taken from Veronica Franco's Capitolo 3, specially translated for this book by the co-author of VERONICA FRANCO: POEMS AND SELECTED LETTER, the lovely and gracious Professor Ann Rosalind Jones © 2013.

Professor Claire-Marie's recitation of "Then the months and years passed by / so that I had to change my style..." and "When we women, too, have weapons and training, / we will be able to prove to all men..." are also from Venetian poetess Veronica Franco from her book POEMS IN TERZA RIMA. Theses translations are taken from VERONICA FRANCO: POEMS AND SELECTED LETTERS edited by Ann Rosalind Jones and Margaret R. Rosenthal, published by The University of Chicago Press © 1998.

This book is dedicated
to The Great Lady,
my grandmother, Helen Orth.
She is the center that holds.

Chapter 1

We all have lies we tell ourselves in order to survive. We breathe life into these lies, set them before our eyes, and see the world through them. We create safety that way, order.

Maybe that's why what I was doing felt so dangerous.

I was trying to see through mine.

I crouched on a half-submerged rooftop and watched as my fingers drifted back and forth through the filmy green water of the former Venetian lagoon. And I tried to feel the truth. I let the electric charge of the coming storm envelope me, rushing cold over the flesh of my exposed face and forearms, flicking sharp fingers up the legs of my cargo pants, up the sleeves, down the neckline of my winter-weave t-shirt until I shuddered in the charge of too much awareness.

But I had to know.

I *would* know. A far off island—marked only by fallen walls and rooftops protruding from the sea—became my focal point as I fought to release what I'd always believed. As I narrowed my world to those distant walls, the clouds above them began to roil, blocking out the early morning sun, casting me in pale darkness. It was in that darkness that I reached down deep, deep into my lie. And beyond it. I reached past the idea of a healthy body so carefully tended for a physically demanding profession. I strained to feel the stark reality of the disease crouched within me, a disease so vile it would send any child I met into a stasis-like coma—forever. Sleeper's Syndrome.

I couldn't feel it.

It wasn't true.

It *was* true.

I'd run the goddamn test myself. I shoved to my feet, my eyes riveted on those clouds as they slammed and billowed out their destruction. Their wind whipped at my clothing, ripped at my long black hair. Even as I closed my eyes against it, my mind spun out into the violence. *The test. That goddamm test. Three flashing red lights and my life is over.* I raked my hair back from my face, fisted my hands there, tossed my head back to face the sky.

And screamed.

A petty indulgence.

It had its price. My foot slipped. I threw my weight forward, but I knew, I knew it was already too late. I couldn't even work up the give-a-shit to flinch. *Fine,* I thought. *If this is how it is going to end, then this is how it is going to end. Just make it go the fuck away.*

My plunge toward the toxic water and jagged masonry jerked to a halt. I registered an ice-cold hand wrapped around my upper arm. Shock sent me scrambling to set my feet under me and I spun around.

"What the hell—"

The snarl dropped from my lips as I looked up into those flat, unblinking eyes on that too-white face. Wet black hair hung down his naked chest; a few strands of it clung to my cheek. My fingers wandered up to brush it away. I stared at it, black satin against my white fingertips.

"You're real," I whispered.

He loosened his grip enough that I could turn to face him fully. His hard alien features did not bend in expression, but I felt sadness seeping from him as he scooped my own hair back from my face. He backed up the roof, drawing me with him.

Short flashes of memory assailed me, half-remembered images of two nights ago, the night I'd died: Desperation as the waves knocked me under. A scream that filled my lungs with the sea. A white and black shark charging with teeth bared. A man, this man cradling me as I died. I raised my hand to his arm.

"Before. You saved my life. You..."

I left the sentence unfinished in case the rest had just been a beautiful dream, fed by an undernourished libido. But then he drew me up to my toes and what I felt matched that dream too perfectly. His cold, hard lips brushed mine, his strong fingers cupped my head, bearing the weight for me. I reached for his tongue with my own, tasted his salty essence as he opened and let me slide into him. So perfect. I leaned against him. His arms wound around me, pulling my shoulders and hips tight against him, protected, safe. For the first time in days I felt the dark coil in me loosen; the tension in my shoulders eased so fast my head floated. All I could do was cling and watch those dark eyes as they stared inside of me, as they drew me up and in until the body I'd just tried so hard to know loosened its hold on my mind.

And was gone.

I was in darkness. But it was not emptiness. I felt him, my shark god, wrapped around me, protecting me from the open wildness around me. Unleashed energy, emotion raged all about us, threatening destruction, creation, explosive life. The sheltering cocoon of him kept me centered in the fierce storm, kept it from ripping me apart. But he couldn't keep me from drinking it into me.

To the point of agony.

I struggled, desperate from the almost-knowing, the almost-understanding. He wouldn't release me to it, wouldn't let me grasp that final ecstasy of comprehension. Instead, he drew me into his calm.

And, impossibly, I did calm. My frantic thrashing settled into a quiet awareness as the sensory immersion artist in me remembered how to switch off any emotion not pertinent to the scene, any outside thoughts skewing the sensations that would tie the audience to the character that housed them. Slowly, the cacophony became a storm's symphony—ecstatically beautiful to behold.

I became the observer, but I sensed the ancient clash with something other than the tools of my profession: my skin, my eyes, my ears, my tongue. I sensed it with the same senses I used to understand the peace in a dappled patch of shade in my beloved woods; the same senses I used to feel the lives that had gone before me as I wandered a forgotten cemetery. Those senses that knew there was something *more*.

Something more. Something more, if I could just reach out, just reach a little further into that bright darkness. Then I would know; I would understand and everything that had seemed so utterly senseless would reveal its meaning with blinding clarity—the death of my father; the loss of my life and my freedom to this disease; the violent indifference of this sunken city. All that awful, beautiful mystery taunting me, it could fill me. All I had to do was fling myself open to it, embrace it with fang and claw and an animal scream. It licked at the edges of me. With its touch, I felt powerful and terrifyingly whole.

The kiss broke.

A chill wind slapped at me. The tiny flicks of pain matched the scattered charges of fear sparking in my chest. Unsteadily, I drew back, looked up at him.

"What did you do?"

I shivered. I could feel residuals of that desperate pull in my arms, my legs, everywhere. It wasn't fading fast enough. It was fading too fast. I was missing something. Something important.

"What just happened to me? What was that?"

My shark god, he just rested his hands on my shoulders and looked down at me with his blank face, but warmth seeped into me from his cold body, warmth and a soft feeling...affection.

He wasn't going to answer me.

"No, you can't mess with me like that, take me apart like that, and then—"

He pressed on my shoulders, directing me to turn. I watched him, wary, but finally curiosity won out and I let him turn me back to face the waters.

My strange guardian kept his hands on my shoulders as we both looked out at the boiling, black clouds lit with lines of electric fire. What did he want me to see? I looked down the length of the ruins, but there was little left. The encroaching sea was too powerful for a small island to stand against alone.

Mo, help me. What is that place?

San Michele, *the island of the dead.*

Island of the dead: a cemetery. I waited. My AI implant knew I needed more than just a mere place name.

San Michele once housed the workshops of the great cosmographer, Father Mauro. Working deep within his convent laboratory, this Camaldulian monk created the greatest piece of Late Medieval cartography known to historians, his mappamundi or map of the world. The famed detail and proportion of the map he humbly attributed to discussions with Venetian navigators, the masters of the sea.

But there were whispers. How could a man who had not traveled to these exotic locations have drawn them with such precision? How could conversation alone lead to mapmaking of so much mastery? Those whisperers looked to the skies above the island and found their answers there in the tearing lines of the lighting, in the fractured shapes of the storm clouds that hovered over the convent. They intimated that the good father had stolen into Lucifer's dreams and projected those dreams onto the dark clouds above the laboratory. They claimed that as Lucifer dreamed his chaos into the world, Father Mauro copied down the shapes of places still unknown even to the sea-faring Venetians. They warned that such manipulation would end in disaster. You see, Lucifer's maps, hidden in the terror of midnight storms, served their own purpose: they guided witches and other unholy beings to their wicked enclaves where they would plot how best to steal souls for their master.

And indeed tragedy struck. Father Mauro's life's work, the great mappamundi, was sent to the man who commissioned it, King Alfonso V of Portugal...and was lost to the negligence of time. Only a mere copy was destined to survive, a copy displaying but a portion of the master's power. Father Mauro died in 1460 before completing the second work.

I sighed in frustration. A map dreamed by the devil. That lingering fear of missing something vital sharpened. I stared ahead and saw only clouds.

But as I watched, the darkness cracked. The morning sun ripped through the split horizon, golden and illuminating below the ceiling of the storm. The sea shimmered in the light and I felt the warmth brush my cheeks. I tilted my face up for more.

His cold hands slid from my shoulders. The marrow in the bones of my shark-bitten arm shot with pain: he was gone. My shark god had slipped back into the sea. But the sun was still with me, clearing my head, sharpening my senses, setting my heart to beating again.

And for the first time in twenty-four hours, I had a thought that wasn't about poor little ol' infected me:

If my shark god was real...

...then those psychotic feral carriers were real, too.

And I'd left Ryan and Ben alone.

Hands shaking, I scrambled back across the tile rooftop.

℘

I reached the window of the old monastery turned military barracks and slowed my steps across the sharply angled rooftop. I had to play this right. Two men noble enough to ride to my rescue when they thought I was wrongfully imprisoned in a Sleeper's Syndrome quarantine camp might not react the right way if I told them the ruins were crawling with murderous Syndrome carriers. I didn't want them to dig themselves in deeper. I wanted to get them the hell out of here.

In the shadows and light of the office we'd commandeered the night before, I saw my cameraman, Ryan Gunner, crouched to the side of a swath of fallen wallpaper, his vaguely Hispanic skin dusted with the ever-present grit of a crumbling city. He bent his short, muscular frame over something shiny on the floor—something that looked deliciously like a space heater. I flexed my fingers, trying to get the blood flowing. God, what I would give to be warm again! Maybe I would be able to stay in this one place long enough to thaw out.

After I convinced them to abandon me here.

My body tried to hesitate.

I didn't let it.

I sat myself down and swung both legs over the window ledge, dropped to the floor. Ryan jumped, that deceptively youthful face hardening, his eyes checking all possible points of entry. He spotted me and relaxed, only to suddenly look exhausted beyond functioning. Strange how we can keep moving and moving until something interrupts that inertia and we realize we just don't have the energy to start it up again. But he did. After a few blinks of his eyes, he set the palm-sized space heater down and the disk between its reflective plates warmed to a red glow. Ryan straightened and walked over to me, dusting his hands off on his pants.

Time to say those words we'd all been avoiding.

"Looks like there's going to be a break in the storm. I can set this stuff up myself. You and Ben should get going," I said.

Ryan opened his mouth, but his reply was cut off by a bellow from the next room.

"Goddamn fucking piece of..." Ben Norris-Stevens, my bodyguard and stunt coordinator, appeared in the doorway tangled in a billow of save-my-ass-yellow made all the more startling with his African-American coloring. God, I hoped that thing was clean or he was going to have the rash from hell.

Ben side-stepped the space heater and tried to shove the half-inflated raft at Ryan. The gesture jerked his head down. He yanked a coil of the inflatable from his neck and shoulders, then dumped the whole pile at Ryan's feet. "*You* get it back in the bag, Army boy."

"Anti-Terrorist Force," Ryan muttered as he knelt to scoop up the silk-like material. "And why the hell should that make me the civilian camping gear expert?"

This was already headed the wrong direction. I snatched the raft from Ryan.

"I'll take care of blowing this up. You two need to get going. There's going to be a break in the storm any minute now. Go ahead and grab your gear. I'll get you set up out there."

I turned toward the window. If they needed momentum, I would give it to them. Off we go, boys. Away from the super-strong, super-violent nutcases I'm going to be rooming with for the rest of my life. A shudder rippled through me. I hid the reaction by hurrying to pile the unmanageable yellow mass onto the windowsill. I'd had to come back to the main island. This was where the food was. But what was I going to do when those black-eyed, feral Syndrome carriers, when their Hadria who'd ordered their hunt figured out I wasn't dead? I'd barely survived one night of them hunting me. Did they change into ferals every night? Every single night?

"Alyse."

I realized I'd quit moving. Immediately, I gathered up the rest of the raft and pinned it to one half of the windowsill. Maneuvering this faux-parachute out there in the wind was going to be a trick.

"Get your shit together, Ben. I don't care how good you think you are with that hand-held, another fog bank like the last one comes in, you'll find yourself somewhere in the middle of the Adriatic being attacked by a mutated squid. Let's go."

"Alyse, we're not going," Ryan said to my back.

Oh, shit. No, no, no.

Slowly, I turned to face the two men.

"At least not yet," Ryan amended.

I studied their faces, both so haggard, both so dear to me. They'd come back for me—something I could never have asked for, had never expected. Something I was still trying to wrap my heart around. I saw the conviction in their faces, saw the tremor in Ben's dark hand.

I chose my words carefully. "No. No, you are going. I appreciate it, but it's best if you go now. I will figure this thing out. I'm a big girl. When I get settled, I will make some calls. Ryan, Britta Niles has always loved your work. It shouldn't be too hard to get you on her crew. Ben, I could probably get you into my old stunt team, if you want. Maybe...maybe I could even find something for Tamsin."

"Maybe later." Ryan walked up beside me, flipped the switch on the inflatable. It hissed as it shrank beneath my hands. In seconds, it was no longer a lumpy wall between us. Carefully, he began to draw the fabric from my grip. I panicked.

"Ryan, you don't understand. You need to go. I need you to go now."

"This isn't just about you anymore, Alyse."

"No, it's not. It's about you. This place isn't safe—"

Ben stepped forward then and I caught myself from blurting out the truth. He settled a hand on my shoulder; his breath shook on the exhale.

"Somebody gone and done this to you, baby. What's stoppin' them from doin' it to somebody else? What's stoppin' them from sending a whole 'nother batch of babies to sleep?"

Ryan looked up from rolling the raft into a tight ball. "The answer's here. If I can get enough data, Booth can open a file on these guys. The ATF can take it from there."

The Anti-Terrorist Force. At least they were known for handling things quietly. Maybe my mother and the rest of my relatives wouldn't have to go down in flames with me. Maybe the rest of the attendees from the meeting that had brought us to the Venetian ruins wouldn't have to suffer because of what had been done to me.

Maybe I could learn who had condemned me with this disease— so I could hunt them down and make them bleed.

"I will find out who did this. There is no reason for you to stay," I said.

"You wouldn't know what to look for," Ryan countered.

"You could tell me."

"I won't know it until I see it."

I straightened and used my full height on both of them. "And I won't let you risk yourselves like this. You are leaving. Now." I grabbed the raft back from Ryan just as he finished sliding the neat bundle into its bag. I grabbed Ben's pack and Ryan's from where they rested against the opposite wall of the barren, tattered room. I twisted to toss Ben's pack out the window. He made a grab for it and nearly jerked my shoulder out of its socket before it tore free. I turned back and got the pack full in the chest.

I stumbled back, rapped my head and back against the stone window frame. The packs and the raft fell to the floor.

"Get it through your goddamn head: We're stayin'. You can't do it by yourself. You're afraid of these people. I ain't never seen you afraid of nobody or nothing. That says somethin' to me, Alyse. That says you need us here to cover your ass, to help you figure out who did this to you...without...you...getting...killed."

The rap to my head was still doing its Doppler run through my skull. I gave my head a shake to cut it off.

"This how white knights operate these days? Save the damsel by cracking her skull?"

"Only if she got one thick as yours."

I laughed despite myself.

Ben walked over and rubbed the back of my head by way of apology. Just that simple bit of contact and my artificial resolve weakened pitifully. Abruptly, I straightened and stepped away. I needed a new tactic.

"A day."

"A week," Ryan replied, his doe eyes dissecting my every micro-expression.

I stared him down. Could I keep them off the radar for that long? Hadria and the whacked out carriers who answered to her thought I was dead. Here in the outer ruins, nobody was likely to stumble across us by accident, but Ryan would want into the Doge's Palace. No, no way this was going to work.

"Too long."

"You're suddenly the expert?"

"Don't try that," I warned. "You've been out of the ATF for almost ten years now. And you don't know this place. If they realize I'm still here, it's over." Translate "it's over" as "we're dead."

I don't know what Ryan saw on my face, but I saw him hesitate. Ben, however, did not.

"This ain't no enactment, baby. You ain't callin' the shots. Army Boy and me, we talked. We're stayin'. Your only call is to help or to keep the hell out of the way."

With that, Ben bent down, hefted the two travel packs and the raft in its bright yellow bag and strode back out of the room.

Quite the dramatic exit.

In the jarring silence that followed, Ryan and I turned to each other. With Ben having put my pompous ass so summarily in its place, I couldn't think of a thing to say. He was right, I wasn't their boss anymore. They weren't answerable to me. I wasn't a...I wasn't an anything anymore. I blinked, didn't give the thought a chance to settle.

Ryan still watched my face, questions flashing behind those eyes. Whatever they were, though, he still wasn't ready to ask.

I felt warmth touch my shoulder. I turned and saw the sun had won the day against the morning storm. For now Lucifer's map had been erased. For now. I felt the rays as a tangible pressure against my numb face, pushing the chill away, gently forcing the life back into me. And then, in that moment, I understood what my silent shark god meant to give me when he showed me the light cracking open the darkness.

Hope. He meant to give me hope.

I lowered my head in acknowledgement.

"Well, Army Boy," I said over my shoulder, "shall we go play whodunit?"

Chapter 2

I struggled to look calm as the three of us huddled in front of the little space heater. The sun had an indirect line on our single window. It would be midday before these stone walls warmed. I shifted closer to the space heater. God, I was sick of being cold!

We had settled on a technological compromise: we would use the control board from Ryan's swarm cameras to compile our research and conclusions for Ryan's ATF friend Booth. Between the three of us we represented the upper three tiers of the technological divide: Ben with his com gear (optical and auditory nerve taps, tooth mike, and motion chips); Ryan with his basic AI able to feed data to and be controlled directly by his brain; and me with the most advanced AI available, exceeding Ryan's military-issued gear with the ability to record all physiological and mental sensation, even the dreams of my twisted, twisted subconscious mind.

And we were using a control board for research.

Because our technologies' greatest strength was its greatest vulnerability: immersion. The user became immersed in the research environment and lost connection with the physical one. That same environment where Hadria's hunters lurked. Even without me blurting out the truth that might keep them from ever leaving, my boys were wary enough to make that concession.

"So we have the what. We need the who, where, when, and why," I said.

Ryan nodded. "I'd have to at least have solid leads on the who and the why in order to turn this over to Booth."

"Dr. Franco suspected the surgery for my immersion gear to be the when and why. I don't. If that were the case, Bryce, Kelsie, and the rest of the immersion artists would have been kept here, as well." I pulled my knees up to my chin and dug my fingers into my shins. This was old territory. I'd beat my brain to a pulp over this for so long already. I needed new information, new possibilities, new perspective. I needed to speed this up. I needed to get these guys out of here.

"Well, whadda we know 'bout this DNA patch itself?" Ben asked.

Slowly, I nodded to him as I sorted it out in my brain. A fresh path. It could go somewhere. "Okay, Franco said it was similar to, but not exactly the same as the ones from his Brighton's Disease group."

Ryan looked up from the control pad balanced on his crossed legs. "Does that mean it's also Sleeper DNA?"

Sleeper DNA. That was the source for the genes that had cured Brighton's Disease, a modern scourge that caused blindness before it turned fatal.

It happened long before my time, but it became big news again when I was in high school—and my dad was in the news business. I remembered him telling me that about twenty years earlier a group of religious fanatics called the Flaming Sword of God had bombed the Cathedral of St. John the Baptist in Turin. He said the terrorists did manage to destroy a holy artifact or two, but they'd unearthed a miracle, too. The bombing revealed a previously sealed underground tomb of Sleepers, people whose clothes were over 1,800 years old, but whose bodies hadn't aged a day. The Turin Project was founded and research began.

The day the Sleepers came back into the news was the day a select group of people with advanced Brighton's Disease underwent a gene therapy program developed from Sleeper DNA. Beyond the expectations of every medical and religious critic, the therapy worked and we all breathed a sigh of relief.

If only the terrorists had left well enough alone.

Finally, I shook my head. "I have no idea if it's Sleeper DNA or not. Dr. Franco never said one way or another." And we probably wouldn't be figuring that out without asking Dr. Franco himself. That kind of data was classified in a way even good ol' Booth probably wouldn't have access to.

"Wouldn't it have to be? I mean, if you went and caught Sleeper's Syndrome, don't you gotta be part Sleeper?" Ben asked, looking back and forth between the two of us.

"If you run with that idea, then that narrows down the when. The Turin Project Research Center was sealed up after the Sleeper's Syndrome outbreak. It means," Ryan continued, turning toward me, "that you were either altered before the outbreak or—"

"—after I got here."

But Ryan promptly doubled back on himself and blew that idea to hell. "Unless someone was working with a stolen sample. Remember? Sleeper's Syndrome itself was released when those Flaming Sword guys broke into the Turin Project and stole one of the Sleepers."

"That's right! That Sleeper chick was never recovered." Ben snapped his fingers, repeatedly as the memory came back to him. "And three of her tomb-mates disappeared like the next night or somethin'."

"Which leaves four Sleepers worth of DNA floating around out there on the black market. We're not going to get a timeline out this side of the equation." I sprang to my feet and started pacing behind them. The bare floorboards beneath my feet shrieked with each step—in time with my nerves.

"We need your medical history," Ryan said.

Good! Perfect! "You can't access that from here. It's on a cube in Dr. Keith's office."

Ryan didn't even turn around to look at me. "Nice try."

Damn. Apparently not that nice.

"Tamsin's back there by now," Ben said carefully.

I stopped pacing. Tamsin. As in Tamsin Leonides, our field producer and my flake of a best friend. As in no way in hell was I asking her for help.

"No."

Ryan set down the control board and got to his feet, too. "Yes."

I saw the hard set of his face and I knew where it came from. His little niece Haylee lay in a stasis-like coma in a Children's Castle in Vermont, her sweet six-year-old face just the same as it had been ten years ago. She was one of the victims of Sleeper's Syndrome. The carrier? Her first grade teacher. The teacher had been lynched three days after the wave of young victims was traced to the recipients of the gene therapy for Brighton's Disease. Sick. The whole thing was sick.

But if I could use this to get even one of these guys on the other side of the Venetian security perimeter, I would do it. I stepped closer.

"She made it abundantly clear that calls from me would not be answered."

Ryan just raised an eyebrow. "You have some bridges to mend, then."

"Perhaps you haven't noticed, but when Tamsin dumps someone, she does it summarily and without looking back."

Behind Ryan, I heard Ben make a rude sound of agreement, but Ryan didn't budge. "She was hurt, she was scared, and she was angry, Alyse."

"Maybe that can excuse what she said, but not what she did."

Ryan didn't answer. He stood there, immovable, waiting for the rest. It was me who finally broke away to stare out the window.

"Talk to her, Alyse."

"No."

"Don't you think she deserves—"

I turned on him. "No! I stood there, in the worst moment of my life—I'd been beaten, drugged, infected with Sleeper's Syndrome, and tossed in prison—and she tells me to fuck off, leaves me, abandons me to the hands of the people who probably purposely destroyed my life. No, I will not call her!"

Ryan's face went pale and Ben shoved to his feet. Looking at the shock on their faces, I realized too late that I'd let too much of the truth slip out. I'd never told them what had happened that night. Ben took a breath, but I held up my hand.

"No, no, don't start. I'll call her. I'll call her."

I circled wide and let my long stride carry me out of the room.

What the fuck did it matter. She wasn't going to answer anyway.

՟

"Alyse! I'm so sorry! I was a total shithead. I've been so awfully worried! Are you okay, honey?"

Tamsin's bob of wavy blonde hair bounced as she ran the words over each other, the pale skin of her face was splotchy and a tear escaped completely unheeded. In the visual Mo projected into my brain, the colorful blankets and throws on the couch behind my best friend told me Ryan was right: She was home. I made myself wait a heartbeat while my head sorted out how to respond. My instant reaction was dual and violent:

I wanted to laugh until I cried. My best friend, my Tamsin, I hadn't lost her, she hadn't forsaken me after all! I'd missed her so much!

I wanted to rip her throat out. Of course she was sorry. She'd made it out; she was safe. And the boys had stayed with me, stood by my side. She couldn't be the bad guy, so of course she hadn't meant what she said. Worst betrayal of my life...simply forgotten.

Later.

Ryan was right. This wasn't just about me anymore.

So I ignored her question and got to the point. "I need your help. I need access to my medical file."

Tamsin blinked, more tears fell. These she rubbed away.

"Um, I...I guess I could talk to Dr. Keith for you." Good, she got the picture: *no, she was not yet forgiven.*

Slowly, I shook my head as I picked my way down a splintered staircase at the end of our hallway.

"No, I don't want Dr. Keith knowing about this." How to be specific without sending up a red flag to The Flaming Sword, The Seers, and every other nut job in the universe? A prior medical condition? Seizures? Would they buy that? Would Tamsin, the queen of the artless con, be able to follow along?

"I'm looking for any record of these seizures happening before."

As I said it, the reason for my hesitations about the doctor became crystal clear. "If they happened before I came here, the doctor would have to have known about it. And she still cleared me for the field. I could have broken my neck out there."

There. Just like telling a story at a bonfire. I paused on what was left of the staircase landing and let it sink in. Tamsin didn't miss a beat.

"Oh, god, you think Dr. Keith..."

"I don't know. I don't want to think that." But, fuck, I didn't want to believe any of this was true.

Tamsin took a deep breath and leaned forward on her couch. "Okay, what exactly am I looking for?"

"Probably nothing you could analyze yourself. We'll have to feed it through an AI to look for markers. Ryan will have to set it up for you, but if you can find my master DNA record, any DNA marker reporting, family medical history, all that. You'll have to look around." I had to trust she remembered Sleepers' Syndrome carriers had gene replacement therapy. Mismatched DNA, Tamsin. We are looking for mismatched DNA.

"I get it, I get it." I saw that con artist gleam in her eye and a traitor of a smile twisted its way onto my face. She clapped her hands together. "I get to go Nancy Drewing! Oh, I always thought I would just make the most spectacular gumshoe! Just you wait, George and Bess, and see what this brilliant mind can deduce."

And she was launched.

I looked down and saw where a hole had been punched into the thick wall just a few paces to my left. As Tamsin forgot her tears in a whirlwind of enthusiasm over her new covert career path, I crawled through the crumbled brick. I emerged onto the remains of a decorative balcony overlooking a cavernous church, the Church of the Gesuiti. Above the greenish sea water, the walls were fringed with a yet darker moss. Rising from the green, the grayed marble—probably once gleaming white—climbed skyward in hacked chunks like the first rough pencil sketches for a cubist painting. Unlike most of the structures I'd been inside, though, the infrastructure of the building was largely intact—surprising considering how close it was to the sea.

"...think of a way to get Dr. Keith to leave the file open when she leaves. Then I can record the data with one of our spare swarm cameras. Now where are those—"

"In my apartment."

"Is your mom still there?"

I stiffened. "Not a word about any of this to my mom."

"Oh, I'd already reckoned that was the case, I just figured I'd tell her we'd forgot a few..."

On the wall opposite from where I crouched, a larger, more stable looking balcony beckoned, probably a pulpit from the days when preaching the gospel didn't get you tackled by officers expecting to pry a detonator from your cold, sweat-slicked hand. Looters had shattered most of the pulpit's green inlaid stone, but I could see how it once would have draped around the speaker like a heavy oriental brocade. The walls around the ornate balcony still showed fragments of the masterful stone working with its damask-style floral pattern.

I surveyed the tumble of fallen marble and stacks of rotted pews that rose from the water below. I could see the hint of a path across the nave of the church. A Vittorio-style path—hidden in plain sight. After following the giant, white-blonde native Venetian, Vittorio, halfway across the city on death-defying trails just like this one, I knew exactly what I was looking at.

"...get into the doctor's billing records. There's always interesting stuff in there. At least in the movies. Of course that might be a little more illegal, but—"

"Tamsin, just stick to the medical records for now!"

"Alright, alright. I suppose you are right, I just thought we could look for shady transactions or out of place—"

"Tamsin!"

I might not be in the mood to listen to Tamsin's external monologue, but I ought to know by now that tuning her out completely could get dangerous. That mind and that mouth could flip from one topic to another faster than I could trip through the sections of this obstacle course.

My battered muscles complained as I lowered myself down to the first chunk of ragged marble, stumbled as it crumbled, just barely caught myself on a dangerously soft plank from an upturned pew. I straightened and took the next three sections of rock and wood a little more carefully. And tried, truly tried to tune into a jarringly cheerful conversation that I was in no way in the mood for.

"...although that's going to be the tricky part, because I'm not sure even I can talk faster than Dr. Keith, but I'll think about it. There's got to be someway to separate her from that lab, maybe a kitty emergency. What *are* you doing anyway, 'Lyse? Your background is blank and your avatar is flailing all over the place."

I reached the underside of the pulpit, felt around the rim, and found what I was looking for: a rope. I wrapped my hand around it and heaved. Miraculously the ancient stone held. I got one, then the other hand up on the balcony wall, then I was up and over. I looked back over the green water and shook my head.

"Just going for a walk—Venetian style."

I sank down into the dusty cocoon of stone and leaned my head back against the wall.

"Venetian style." Tamsin hesitated. "So you're still there, but if I can find your medical records...but you think..."

I turned my head toward a missing chunk of the pulpit wall, watched the lapping water as it swayed back and forth nourishing the moss, destroying the eighteen-hundred-year-old city it had once cradled and protected from the violence of the world beyond.

"Let's just say that while you're breaking into my apartment, you can feel free to lift anything you like."

"You won't be coming home."

"No." Edit that. I had to edit that, before my temper got us all killed. "The doctors said no travel permitted."

"Oh, God, 'Lyse."

"Yeah, well, whatever. Just let me know how your life of crime goes. This needs to happen quickly. Ryan and Ben won't leave until we've figured out what happened to me. I can't have them...."

"But Ben and Ryan said you weren't—"

"Well, congratulations. You were right; they were wrong."

Tamsin flinched and the tears started up again. Okay, that was mean. But her transitory pain, her easy flips between cheer and distress—I couldn't deal with them right now. I wanted to grab her and shake her, scream at her, *This is real! Can't you take something seriously for once in your life! I will not be just another flash of meaningless emotion for you—there, then gone. Just completely gone.* I swallowed it down—hard. Not about me. Not about me.

"Look," I closed my eyes and pressed a fingertip to my forehead. "I'll get over it. Just help me get these guys out of here. Please." I looked up and had to push away tears of my own. "If anything happened to them, I couldn't, I couldn't...not after losing Dad. I couldn't. You have to help me get them out of here."

I saw the fear creep into my best friend's eyes, but amazingly she didn't ask any questions. Maybe she knew me better than I thought.

"Alrighty, I'll call when I get the data."

"Thanks, Tamsin."

"I love you, Alyse."

I sighed, then raised my head to look her in the eye. "I love you, too."

And I meant it.

Later.

⁊

I woke with my head crammed between the wall and a fallen piece of stone drapery I didn't remember being there when I arrived. Cautiously, I pulled myself upright, scraped a nice crust of crumbled rock from the side of my face.

"Crap."

Ben and Ryan were going to think I'd gotten my dumb ass stranded somewhere with a broken leg.

You have one message.

Shit. Open it.

But it wasn't Ben. It was Bryce Deacon, the male sensory immersion artist for Lone Pine Pictures, my partner and my ex. His message was short and simple as he stood there looking at me with those hooded cobalt eyes, worrying the bone pendant that hung by a piece of hemp twine from his neck:

"Call me, Alyse. Let me know you're alright. I...I already know you didn't make it out. I can help you. You can trust me, Alyse. Call me. Please."

He hung his head and that sweep of blonde hair fell forward over his eyes. The message ended.

My mind went blank forever. But the icy ache in my chest outstripped even that emptiness. I raised my hand, pushed back the horrible pain between my breasts. I was never going to get to fix that, never going to get the chance to really understand how a connection that bright and vivid had become an ending that dark and destructive. Less a hole in my heart, more like filaments of my soul torn away—now never to be restored. How many years had I wasted hiding, protecting myself from him? *You can trust me, Alyse.* I pressed my eyes into my knees and hissed out the pressure of the tears that were never going to fall.

"God."

In the huge cavern of the gutted church my single word came back to me. The irony pulled a broken chuckle from my throat. I raised my head, forced my eyes to see the cracked ceiling extending at least a full story above me. If this was supposed to be a sanctuary, I didn't feel comforted. I'd never entirely understood these places; they were built so huge, made you feel so small. I'd heard people say it was to make you feel small, humble before God, but I only felt small and maybe a little bit frightened before the wealth and power of the human machine that had created these opulent, yet austere chambers. Did millions in paintings make a place more sacred than Grandma Anala's cluster of willows by the stream?

Actually, there were some who said it was solely Titian's Martyrdom of St. Lawrence *that made this place worth entering at all.*

I jumped at Mo's abrupt interjection, then winced as she showed me a haunting, yet highly romanticized painting of a man with perfect abs being barbecued on a giant grill as his persecutors balletically stoked the flames and the light of God looked on from a break in the clouds high above.

Gruesome. They certainly were creative in those days.

St. Lawrence actually met his end in 258 during a Christian purge by Valerian. St. Lawrence was an adherent of Pope Sixtus the Second and is said to have seen the Romans hauling his holy father off to face the executioner's axe. St. Lawrence is recorded to have called out to the Pope, "Where are you going, my dear father, without your son? Where are you hurrying off to, holy priest, without your deacon? Before you never mounted the altar of sacrifice without your servant, and now you wish to do it without me?" Wherein, the Pope is said to have prophesized, "After three days you will follow me."

I grimaced. That wasn't a prophesy. The Pope probably knew Lawrence well enough to know he was going to do something stupid.

Perhaps. Lawrence was then given three days to gather the Church's wealth and deliver it to the Romans. And perhaps because he already knew those three days were to be his last, he took that time to distribute that wealth among the poor. Then on the third day, he collected the poor and the suffering from his flock and presented them to the Romans as the "jewels" of the Church, saying that in them "the Church is truly rich, far richer than your emperor."

Just had to have the last word, didn't he?

Oh, but that was not the last word. Martyred as he was on the gridiron, his last words of defiance were "Assum est, inquit, versa et manduca."

Which means?

This side's done. Turn me over and have a bite.

Oh, Mo... that was...that was... But I laughed anyway—which I suspected was the point of her interjection in the first place.

As I looked over the painting, though, the sensory immersion artist in me filled in the agony of the burned flesh tearing away from the superheated metal, the terror of the impossible heat of the flames, the rending disbelief that your fellow man could truly find justification enough to do this to your body.

It hit a little too close to home.

I rubbed my hand over my eyes as Bryce's plea echoed though my brain: *I can help you.*

"Just because I got my head chopped off doesn't mean you have to do anything stupid. Please, Bryce, please don't do anything stupid."

I sighed and hauled myself to my feet. For someone who had just awoken from a catnap, I felt only loosely connected to consciousness. I flexed my hands, my arms just for the reassurance that they would hold. Then I swung over the marble railing and lowered myself down to the apex of a broken wooden box, probably the confessional. I would call him—eventually.

But one emotional evisceration a day was my limit.

And I already had one set of martyrs on my hands.

Rusty nails and warped, misaligned floor boards heralded my return to our little camp in what remained of the monastery/ barracks.

Ryan and Ben looked up as I came in. I played along with the careful lack of censure on their faces and let the space heater lure me to a seat on the floor next to Ryan. My swarm operator—my *former* swarm operator—picked up the control board and began rapping on it. He handed me the board in an awkwardly formal gesture; he couldn't seem to figure out what to do with his eyes. How did you deal with someone who wasn't an anything anymore? I couldn't give him an answer for that one. I took the board and kept my eyes to myself.

"Ben found some pictures of the Tomb of the Sleepers," Ryan told me. "This one is from the original excavation, before they built the research facility over the top of it."

The image showed a round stone cavern with two tiers of benches cut into the walls. Each bench contained a man or woman arranged in serene repose, the once rich colors of their long tunics, veils, belts, and brooches smothered in a thick layer of dust.

At the center of the room three Sleepers lay separate from the rest. I zoomed in on them.

Mo, what can you tell me about these three?

The Turin project researchers dubbed them The Royals. The center subject, named Princess, was the primary research subject from whom the Brighton's Group samples were taken. The public in their romantic furor called her Sleeping Beauty. After the Flaming Sword terrorists stole her from the research center, her adoring public found cause to change their loving name. Mere hours outside the city, the band of terrorists vanished from the satellite surveillance in the middle of a tree-lined road headed toward the sea.

And then the children began to drop off to sleep.

And Sleeping Beauty became The Witch.

Their faces were so dramatic, even in rest. Under the dust, the man appeared to have a glorious head of long blonde hair, high, hard cheekbones, full lips—joy and radiance seemed to hide under that kingly stillness. The queen had a smaller, harder body. The sharp lines of her face seemed almost crafty, leaning towards a cruel beauty. As for the princess, it wasn't hard to see why the world had fallen in love with her. Her dark hair lay in soft curls around a soft, sweet face.

"There are other pictures."

Ryan reached across and tapped the board. This image was from inside the tomb itself. "This is during the construction of the research facility."

"The king is gone."

Ben leaned back behind all of us to snag a daypack from against the wall. "Yeah, don't remember if he was 'disappeared' or if he was just the first human pincushion."

I didn't either—too long before my time. I asked Mo. To my surprise she didn't produce an immediate response. I took the bag Ryan passed me. I reached in and felt the waterproof liner of the bottom. After a couple of sweeping gropes, my fingers found an energy bar. One energy bar.

Media reports declare the king the first test subject.

Caught up in my new worry, it took me a moment to remember what my question had been.

"Mo says the king was the first test subject," I relayed. "Is this really the last one?" I waved the bar at Ben.

"Yes, ma'am."

I flipped through the rest of the pictures: now both the princess and the king were missing—Brighton's research had begun; now the queen and two of her courtiers left the stage—Sleeper's Syndrome ravaged the earth. Five empty biers or benches or whatever they were called. Five possible sources of the threat I posed. Who the hell had those five bodies? And how were they connected to me?

The location of the four Sleepers is unknown. The fifth, the king, is presumed to be located in the sealed labs of the Project Facility. The connection to you is unknown.

Rhetorical, Mo.

I handed Ryan back the board and began to strip the wrapping off of our very last energy bar. It looked so small—and inedible.

"We, uh, I found a couple of connections between Dr. Keith and Dr. Franco." Ryan spun the control board between his palms and finally, finally looked at me. "They were both at a conference in Amsterdam two years in a row—just a couple years before your surgery, just a couple of years before Sleeper's Syndrome. They were speakers. Bio-tech conference."

A little electric jolt ran the length of my sternum. But. "But they are both big names in bio-tech, so that doesn't necessarily..."

"No, but I think the best we can do right now is start generating a list of possible connections and start crossing it off as we can. They knew each other. That's a connection."

I dropped my head with a nod, chewed my way through a particularly large bite of protein-packed nastiness. Ben tossed his wrapper in my direction, in the direction of the daypack.

"That's only gonna last this boy an hour, two tops."

"I know where there's food." I knew where there was food. I knew where there was a pretty little grocery store, run by a sweet little homicidal maniac named Anna.

"Good." Ben pushed to his feet, dusted off his pants. "Then lets take us a lil' break and go raid the palace."

I'd never moved so fast. I jumped up and cut him off.

"No."

Ryan had already set the control board aside. He froze midway through tucking his feet underneath him.

"Alyse, no matter how long we stay we're going to have to set up a stock pile—"

"No, no one can see you. No one can suspect you are here. There is a grocery in their sort of town square thing. I will handle

this. I know how to get in and out of there." I held up a hand.
"Ben, we both know I won't be leaving this place. If I get caught, it
was inevitable. You two...you two...I'm not risking, so just sit back
down and keep poking at that board. I'll be back in about two
hours. Maybe three."

As Ben and Ryan exchanged glances, Ryan finished standing
up. They turned back to me and Ryan nodded.

"I think that might be a good idea. But I need a map and a
promise that you will stay in contact."

I didn't wait for an explanation. Before he could change his
mind, I jogged back to our sleeping room. I found my daypack
and upended it in the least mildewy spot I could find. As I listened
to heated murmurs in the next room, I wrapped my most precious
possessions—the high-tech multivitamins Matteo had sent me—in
the fur blanket from Vittorio's raft hideaway. That tear drop
pendant he'd sent with the vitamins...it still glittered in the darkness
between my breasts. Just for a second, I pressed my fingertips to it,
felt the sharp edges leave their mirror impression in my flesh
through the barrier of my shirt. My heart stuttered, unsure whether
to squeeze in fear or in sorrow.

I dropped my hand.

Time to go.

"...you aren't her bodyguard anymore, Ben."

Just a phrase, a short, simple string of words, but it hooked me
by the gut, tried to reel me back from the window ledge that
beckoned me. How many long, amazing years had we been
inseparable? Day and night, over how many continents? I took a

deep breath, reached deep inside and pulled that barb free. Choked on the pain.

I had to get them out of here.

§

My own sweat plastered my clothing against my skin as I dropped against the moisture-softened wall of a room overlooking what had once been the Campo Santa Marina. I pulled my soggy cargos free of my knees and bent over to recapture my rasping breath. The support wall behind my butt vibrated with the violence of construction.

"A half kilometer away, huh, Mo?"

That is correct.

"Good god!" I wheezed. More like a half kilometer of parkour where most of the surfaces to jump from and to land on teetered on the verge of collapse. At least I'd found one of the native Venetian's "paths" for part of it or it would have taken a hell of a lot longer than an hour and half to get here.

I risked a peek out the naked window.

Seven or eight carriers milled around the tidy town square. They drank rich, dark coffee. They took neat bites of salty meats wrapped in fluffy, melt-in-your-mouth bread. Non-homicidal things. I presumed. I couldn't see their eyes from this distance, couldn't be sure.

I watched their movements from the shadows. The man at the patio table in front of the gleaming coffee shop window set down his tablet. I watched his hairy hand reach for his glass of water. I watched those thick fingers curl around that glimmering cylinder. Was that movement more animal-like, more fluid than...

I let out a breath and dropped my butt to the floor.

Calm. It. Down.

This time when I forced my weary legs beneath me, I trained my eyes exclusively on Anna's little yellow grocery with its quaint dark green awnings. The second story window. The food. The place I'd nearly fallen and brained myself on the cobblestone pavers right below that cute little white flower box.

No albino giant to catch my dumb ass this time.

Rather rely on a hook and a rope anyway. At least it wouldn't fucking run away every time I got in its freaking line of sight.

I refastened the straps on my climbing gloves and then retrieved the length of rope I'd lifted from the construction supplies downstairs. Slipping down the hallway, I headed toward the stairs.

The warped boards of the steps announced my every shift of weight with their own shrill symphony. I let the grinds and thumps of the power tools act as my conductor, measure by measure, taking steps three at a time with each dip of their baton. Shriek, bang—three steps. Shriek, bang-bang-bang—six more steps. Shriek, bang-bang, bang-bang, bang-bang—a whole flight. I ducked behind the banister and peered down the central hallway. A woman in thick overalls lifted a panel of sheetrock and carried it into the furthest room.

The hallway is to the left? I asked Mo.

That is correct.

I took a deep breath. I sprinted for it.

I had to slam myself against a wall.

Just beyond deep afternoon shadows cast by the open doorway, a man walked past. I held my breath as he paused, turned. And then I lost that breath. It was him: the balding Asian who had drug me from that cupboard, who had tried so viciously to strangle me with the scraps of my own shirt. Yesterday.

Oh, god.

I couldn't move, couldn't breathe as he peered past me into the hallway.

I stared out of the corner of my eye. He stepped closer. My mind couldn't process what it saw. He looked so...normal. Just a pudgy, old business man. He looked haggard, cut up, bruised. Broken.

The man sighed and rubbed his hands over his face.

Then he turned.

And left.

Like an iron cast had fallen away from my entire body, my muscles, my lungs reanimated. I shook. God, I couldn't react like this when I saw them. I couldn't just freeze. It put the boys in danger. It could get me killed.

I crouched and readied my rope and hook, forced my hands to steady as I straightened the rope.

Now.

With only a quick glance down the alley, I dashed into the open and threw the hook as I went. I yanked and heard the ancient nails in the windowsill complain at the tension. Using my momentum, I mounted first the window box, then the downstairs windowsill. I shifted my grip up a story, cinched a knotted section of the rope between my feet and launched. I landed my torso easily on that second sill. I slid inside.

See how simple that could have been, Vittorio? Jackass.

Quickly, I gathered the rope up behind me.

I turned around. Food. I scanned the stacks of boxes, the counters, and cabinets. My stomach growled and I grimaced. I needed to get back sooner than later. If my stomach was complaining, my AI and my medic would be soon to follow. I found a crate of energy bars, swung my pack around and started stuffing it. Anna would blame the Venetians. After all, I'd drowned in the Adriatic.

Apples, oranges, anything I could find that didn't require refrigeration.

Water.

"Need a bag for that?"

I froze.

Carefully, I straightened. At the top of the stairs stood a sweet, petite blonde...Cirena's Anna. Shit.

"They said you were dead," she said.

"Are you going to tell them different?"

She stepped forward. I stepped back.

She smiled sadly, then turned aside and walked over to the washbasin that stood under the window overlooking the courtyard. There she paused, her back to me, staring beyond the glass. In her gentle tidiness, she should have stood at the sink of a quaint cottage, admiring her swaying flower garden.

"I won't have to," she murmured.

I smiled bitterly, knowing she was right.

She turned back to me and this time I held my ground as she approached with a tote from the counter. Grocery Girl looked different surrounded by the cold autumn sunlight from the window, glittering, radiant, regal. Everywhere except her eyes. There, where she should have shone, lurked darkness, despair so deep, so fragile it wrenched my heart, despite the cautious adrenaline pulsing through me.

She was barely holding on.

"Anna..."

Those eyes silently begged me not to break her with kindness.

I dropped my shoulders in acquiescence.

She handed me the tote and stepped back. I took the invitation, filling it with water bottles until my arm protested the weight. She walked away. When she returned, she dropped a couple boxed coffees in the side pocket.

I looked up from the gesture.

"I will pay for all this."

"Don't. They'll just find you sooner."

And it had finally been said aloud. They *would* find me. Sooner. Or later.

I let my gaze fall away. What would that mean? Would Hadria with her mysterious hatred turn the city to madness again? Would she send her feral carriers to flush me from the shadows? Or would Jürgen lure me in, imprisoning me under his control the way he had Matteo?

Matteo.

Guilty fear stuttered through one shoulder and out the other. Intellectually, I now understood that he'd no more meant what he'd done to me than Anna had. Intellectually. Someone had ripped his mind away. And now we both had to live with the consequences. All my rage, my fear and grief finally found focus: Hadria. Somehow, someway, before they took me down, she would pay. For the irreparable despair in Anna's eyes, for the pleading horror on Matteo's face. She would pay.

But first things first.

I hitched up my pack, slung the tote over my shoulder. With a nod, I turned from Anna and headed for that cursed window that had stolen so much of my flesh. Just as I dropped the rope over the sill, I hesitated.

"Matteo...is he..." I faltered, not sure exactly what or how to ask.

"Matteo? Matteo who?"

Surprised, I looked back over my shoulder.

"Matteo Ranier. He works in Jürgen's office."

Anna shook her head. "Never heard of him."

I marked the twitch at the corner of her mouth, the funny shrug of her eyelid. My innocent little Grocery Girl was a very bad liar.

Confirmed, Mo agreed with a sweep of her databases.

The bell for the front door downstairs jangled. Anna grabbed the excuse to escape my disbelief. For a split second, I watched her go.

Why would she lie?

Chapter 4

The darkness fell.

The ferals rose.

I couldn't see them yet, but I heard their screams, that primal hunting call: that wild growl that grew and grew until it exploded into a roar, then rose and rose until it split into that two-toned scream of a bird of prey. That piercing scream ricocheted through the city, pinning me to my corner of black night. I crouched further into the moon's shadow cast by the thick stone of the sill, watching my boys sleep.

I will keep you safe.

You have to stay safe.

Clouds drifted past the over-bright moon as if I watched an old under-cranked Hong Kong movie over my shoulder. Those hunting screams seemed to coalesce now, gathering into a pack of focused rage. Beyond Ryan, Ben tossed, his hand batting at something from his dreamscape.

Closer.

I should wake the boys, get them moving. But I so desperately didn't want this to be part of their reality. Maybe I could draw the ferals away from this place, somewhere more toward the palace...

Silence.

Oh...shit.

The air crashed from my lungs as the first one slammed into my back. The rotted wood scraped my cheek where we landed next to Ryan's sleeping form. Ryan didn't stir. I screamed, the monster on my back tearing at my hair, my clothes with clawed fingers. I tried to force a knee free of his pin. I couldn't move my legs under that immense weight. I flung my head back, but the man's face was too far away.

I heard my shirt rip, felt fire across my back. I smelled blood. It was mine.

A huge hand slammed my face back to the floor. I stared at the peaceful expression on Ryan's sweet baby-face. Why didn't he move? Why didn't he wake up? Was he already dead? Was I too late?

"No," I begged, "please no. Not you, too!"

෴

I jerked my eyes open. The shadowed depths of night didn't hold enough reality to flush the nightmare away. Imagined pain still tore at my back, real tears still chilled my cheeks.

They'll just find you sooner.

"Oh, god."

I clamped a hand over my mouth to mask my hitching breaths. I couldn't keep it quiet. I jumped to my feet with my fur blanket and slipped into the next room as silently as I could. In the darkest corner, I buried myself with my blanket and rocked as the sobs and the memories tangled violently in my chest.

Jürgen loomed over me in his terrible majesty, offering me safety if I would only relinquish my soul to him. Promising, promising to protect me if I would obey him in all things.

Matteo's hands glided over my skin, releasing me from the loneliness, releasing me into ecstasy. Seizing my life, my body and dashing it against the end table, shattering all of me.

My father's remaining eye on his mangled face gazing up at me, that beautiful blue like the ocean he so loved. Staring up at me, a window to wordless agony, sucking the love, the joy from my veins slowly, so slowly until the whir of the machines finally died.

Died.

A weight settled on my hair.

I jumped, striking out blindly.

"Alyse. Hey, hey it's just me."

A black silhouette crouched over me. I saw no features. But that voice, that voice.

Even as I drew comfort from the sound, I drew away from him.

Go away! I begged. *Please just go away!*

I didn't dare explain these tears. Not to him.

Ryan made a quiet humming sound. "Did you just have Mo message me to go away?"

I stared at him in confusion. I scraped at the tears I knew shone on my face. Then it clicked: Stupid, clueless, AI. Sweet little Mo. Never quite getting it. Kind of like her owner.

"No. Sorry."

Ryan twisted to sit down beside me.

He settled back against the shriveled wallpaper and wrapped his arms loosely around his knees. Like some kind of criminal caught in the act, I tried to blot and sniff away the evidence of my little meltdown. Ryan just waited, saying nothing, his shadow profile staring off into the intersection of grey moonlight at the center of the room.

The night became silent save for the small sounds of the water in the distance. I tried to absorb that rhythmic silence, displace the guilt and the grief. My eyes burned with the weight of it all and I closed them, leaning my head against the corner.

"You never cried."

My eyes protested as I opened them in surprise.

"What?"

"At your dad's funeral. You never cried. We worried. Tamsin wanted to force you to go to a counselor. I told her to wait, to give you time. Was I wrong?"

Tamsin was the one who wanted to force an intervention? I blinked at him, my cheeks heating.

"You're crying now." He turned to look at me, searching for my eyes in the darkness. "What happened, Alyse? What did they do to you?"

I opened my mouth, but nothing came out.

What did they do to me? Wasn't it enough to know that they had taken my life away? Did he really need the nasty little details of how?

"Alyse...I saw your footage. That guy and his little gang at the dock almost killed you. And their eyes...."

My breath cut off and I gripped his arm over his jacket sleeve.

"Please tell me you didn't tell Ben. Tell me!" I whispered frantically.

Ryan watched me. I drew my hand away. These were not the kind of conversations the two of us had. My stomach practiced its double back flips as I waited for his response. Finally, he shook his head.

"I didn't. I watched the footage when the two of you were sleeping back on the beach. Just bits and pieces. None of it made any sense and I only had a few minutes, but Alyse, what the hell was going on?"

"I...They..." This was exactly what I didn't want my boys knowing, the exact thing that I feared so badly would keep them here when I needed them to go. When I needed them safe.

"Alyse, I have to ask: Did you hit your head hard during any of this?"

That stopped me.

"Grafting?" I asked, just to confirm. As if he could mean something else.

"I saw those files: the black eyes, the way they moved like animals, fluid like wild cats. That kind of stuff just isn't real."

I took a dizzy pause. He thought getting banged around had loosened my AI, freeing it to tap into parts of my brain where it wasn't supposed to be, scrambling my perceptions, interfering with my physical functions.

Killing me.

I blew out a breath, ran my hands briskly over my shins, squeezed my aching calves with each individual finger. I felt fine, my head felt clear. Could grafting be as invisible to the victim as

Sleeper's Syndrome? Would there be no signs that the machine had taken over?

I replayed the last three days in my head. Alone with the carriers and the Venetians and the monsters. No one from my team to verify my surreal flight. How much had that first victim, Carl, suspected before he collapsed in a convulsing heap at his partner Kelsie's feet?

"Alyse, you are thinking really loud."

I jumped.

Ryan ran his hands through his short hair. "Geezus, Alyse! I know that look on your face. I saw it a hundred times back in the ATF. What the hell did they do to you?" And then he paused, seemed to realize something. "How did you *really* end up in that hospital? You said something about prison. You said...you said you'd been beaten...and then those things, those people...."

The more he pieced together, the louder my heart pounded in my brain. I shook my head violently, silently shouting at him to stop!

Ryan's shadow shifted then, scooted back, turned to face me.

"Hey." What was this voice? This was not Ryan's voice. I shuddered at the authoritative kindness, the understanding professionalism. This was not my Ryan's voice. This was their Ryan's voice—Ryan from the ATF hostage evac team. Only he would put such a firm hand on my shoulder, dip so low to catch my eyes.

"Hey," he repeated. "I'm not going to push anymore, Alyse. Let it go. Just breathe through it." Where did that weird shriek in my lungs come from? I held my breath to smother it.

He shook his head at me. "No, breathe."

I forced my breath to sound natural.

I was going to suffocate.

"I'll be here when you are ready to talk."

Not if I could fucking help it.

I nodded.

"I'm going back in the other room. Give you some space."

He pulled his hand away from my fur blanket, away from me. Shifting his weight to his feet, he rose, then walked to the doorway. He paused.

"I do need to know about your head, though. Just a nod yes or no."

That bob of my head felt like a guilty plea.

He sighed. "I'll look into it tomorrow. Try to sleep, Alyse."

I just stared at him, willing him to go. Finally, he did.

I waited until the squeal of the floorboards revealed that he was settling back into his sleeping bag. My breath squealed with them as I tried to recapture so much lost oxygen. I raised my hands to the edge of the moonlight. They shook.

I balled the right one and drove it into the moldy press board next to me.

Goddamn it!

How much longer did I have until I was useless to them? Even if I wasn't grafting, I sure as hell was in the middle of a goddamn nervous breakdown. I took another swing at the wall just to have that impact, just to shut up the goddamn tremors. Ripping away the blanket, I jumped to my feet. The cold bit at me and for the first time in days I didn't care. I rushed at the naked window, grabbed the upper sill, and swung through.

The real moon shone just as shockingly bright as the one from my nightmare. I braced my feet on the tiles of the roof and tossed my head back to face it. In the distance, faint as a whisper, but unmistakable, I heard a feral raise its voice, crying out for the hunt. My lungs contracted with the need to answer. The silver of the moonlight danced along my skin with the skittering sparks of cold.

That kind of stuff just isn't real.

But it felt real. It felt more real than the relentlessly ambitious life I now felt jarringly disconnected from. Sensory immersion artist. Patching together stories, pushing my body and mind to their limits. How much did it matter that I had lived life to its lees, if this is how I ended—at the expense of everyone I'd ever cared about?

Back in high school history class, the story called him the Fallen Prince of Flathead.

I raised a trembling hand to dance my fingers through the moonlight. John Clifford, his light had danced in the hour of becoming. He built a town on the Montana frontier: Demersville. The champagne flowed and the admiration of the townsfolk had lifted him to the heights of mayor. But when the coming railroad chose another path, that town died. Utterly.

And Clifford had allowed his light to die with it.

Drinking turned to attacks on his wife, turned to theft, turned to imprisonment.

So many bright possibilities extinguished.

Because he allowed it.

I withdrew my hand from its dancing. Whatever short time I had left, I would not use it to extinguish the dreams of my friends. Nightmares and trembling hands be damned.

All of our research and we had nothing. They would find me sooner or later.

I'd never been one for sitting around waiting.

Dropping to press my palms against the smooth chipped tiles, I released myself to my body's pressing need to run, to hunt. I sprang forward into the night. Grocery Girl lied. Grocery Girl knew something, something about Matteo, something about me.

And she would be telling those things to an agent of the ATF, a man with a quiet, confident voice, a man whose mind was not potentially corrupted by an invading machine.

ও

The dark still settled heavily on the small campo of Santa Marina when the key stopped working the lock on the door of the cheery little grocery store. I rose from the stool at the register and stood in the crack of dim light from the plaza lamp. She froze before her hand reached the light switch.

"Anna Parks, I will be needing you to come with me."

People used to say I was intimidating.

Anna took one look at my eyes and backed away from the door.

She didn't even try to outrun me.

Chapter 5

"Alyse! Where the freakin' hell'd you go and get off to?"

Ben shoved off the orange and blue sleeping bag he'd bundled himself in and jumped to his feet, looking wild-eyed and scruffy. Ryan set the control panel to the side and eased himself to standing. His quiet eyes watched me. It was to him I spoke.

"I would like to introduce Anna Parks, the owner of the local grocery store here in the camp. She knows something. Since my faculties are currently suspect, I've brought her here to speak with you directly."

I gestured for Anna to enter into the room. She took a hesitating step forward, fear vivid in her wide, soft eyes. I ignored the guilt that had me close to vomiting now that the rage had passed. My hands still shook. I stuffed them into the pockets of my cargos. I had faith in my boys. They would take that fear out of her eyes.

And they would get her to talk.

Ben gaped at her and then at me, rubbed his hands over his rough face and then tried again.

"Ah, Anna, please come in. Can I get you some water or something?"

I watched her shake her head as I stepped back out of the conversation. Ryan shot me a sharp look, but I just answered him with an arched brow. He wanted answers? I brought him answers. And goddamn, but let those answers be enough to turn the inquiry over to Booth, because a missing Grocery Girl would put an idiot on alert. And Jürgen Phan Mai was no idiot.

"Wait. Faculties are currently suspect? Does that mean what I think it means? Now we think Alyse's gonna to go all Carl Loren on our asses?" Ben shot Anna a glance and quickly backpedaled. "I mean, on us. On *us*."

Anna stole a peek at me in confusion. I offered no expression in reply. As I'd hoped, Ryan stepped forward.

"Ms. Parks, my name is Ryan Gunner and this is Ben Norris-Stevens." He reached out to shake her hand and she automatically responded only to hesitate just before contact.

"Dang, girl! What did you go and do to those hands?" Ben stepped around Ryan and flipped her hands over. Even I winced. Better to ask what Venice had done to her hands. "Come on over here and let's get somethin' on those little things."

Ryan took the chance to message me.

Knows something?

Enough to lie to me about knowing Matteo.

Important why?

Matteo is one of Jürgen's inner circle as far as I can tell. If the carriers know something...why else would she lie?

I glanced over to where Ben had pulled Anna aside to hover over her like a giant clucking hen. Anna blushed from ear to ear as he gently cleaned her tiny hands with antiseptic wipes. I turned back to Ryan.

It would be better if I left the room, I think.

We'll take care of her. Try to sleep. I'll let you know what we find out.

I nodded and turned back to the other room, stopping only to snag a sleeping bag.

Alyse?

I paused at the threshold.

Yeah?

I looked it up. There is no definitive test for grafting other than a brain scan.

I kept my face turned away from him as I tensed my muscles against the cold fire that flashed across my flesh. I held my breath as I forced it to subside.

With one hand on the doorframe, I straightened and continued my way deliberately into the other room. With steady, deliberate movements I arranged myself in the sleeping bag. And with deliberate blankness I settled myself for sleep.

Too bad that deliberate blankness couldn't last.

෨

I awoke to the sounds of laughter.

My anger rose in equal and opposite proportion.

I reminded myself that this was what I wanted. It didn't help.

I batted my way free of the blanket and skulked as quietly as I could to where my things lay piled. In the dimming light, I did my best to freshen up and finger-combed my hair back in to a straight-swinging ponytail. As I pawed irritably through the pile for a hair tie, I found the two bottles of tech vitamins Matteo had smuggled me via Luciana. I gave up on the ponytail and stared down at them.

I could ask Mo.

Of course she could only sense what I could sense—which was nothing. And Margie had a fail-safe preventing her little nanobots from penetrating my brain, so she couldn't tell me anything. Or maybe...

Mo, could you ask Margie if my central nervous system is functioning properly?

I felt the stab in my ribs and then the slow spreading fire as my onboard medic started its exam. *Ah, stupid!* Quickly, I popped the caps off the bottles and dry swallowed the pills. I dropped to my butt and lowered my head, choosing to breathe through the pain rather than postpone the diagnosis. I knew this wouldn't give me anything conclusive, but if signals were getting where they were supposed to, I couldn't be too messed up.

Sweat beaded up on my face despite the cold and not all of it was because of the undernourished 'bots. Those vitamins took approximately ten seconds to wreak havoc on my empty stomach. Just a few more minutes...

I could tell by the sound and the sag of the floor that someone heavy had come up behind me: Ben.

"Hey, baby. You doin' okay?"

I held up a finger without looking up. He crouched beside me. One look at my face and he snorted.

"You took those things on an empty stomach?"

He retreated from the room and came back with an energy bar. Oh, yay, another energy bar. Just the thought of choking another one of those things down...made me feel absolutely no different. Ben sat down next to me, peeled back the gleaming wrapper, and offered it to me. Resigned, I accepted it and gingerly nibbled off one corner.

"You usin' Margie?"

I nodded.

"What for?"

I breathed forcefully out my nose, then risked an answer: "Grafting."

"What? Margie can't fix that."

I shook my head. "Test—" Nope! Talking: bad idea. Quickly, I took another nibble of the bar, then pushed a hand over my mouth. Come on stomach. Almost there!

I could feel the fire receding back to my ribs. My muscles ached and cramped in that way that revealed what they'd sacrificed to the hungry little demons conducting my experiment.

"Testing. Got it. Hey, that Anna chick you brought over, she's cool. She's from Alaska. I got a cousin in Alaska. Isn't that where your grandma is, too? She said you'd be less bitchy if we got you some plants. I told her you were always bitchy."

I snapped a hand out and slapped him on the shin.

"Hey, just bein' honest!"

I pulled out another wipe and cleaned my face up again. Then I turned to him with a half-smile. "Yeah, she's good people. I need to go talk to her for a second."

I chewed a mouthful of nasty, sticky, disgusting peanut butter-flavored chemicals as I followed Ben into the next room. Anna, looking happy and relaxed, shared a sliced apple on the floor with

Ryan. When she saw me, her eyes darkened ever so slightly. I took what I deserved.

"Anna, I owe you an apology. My temper got the better of me last night. I've been nothing but beaten and lied to the entire time I've been here and when I realized you were lying to me too..."

"It's only going to get worse."

And I knew she meant all of it. I acknowledged with a nod.

Margie detected no new irregularities in your central nervous system.

I processed this for a minute, then looked to Ryan. "Margie couldn't find anything wrong with my nervous system. That's the best I can do without a brain scan."

Ryan shook his head. "Those files made no sense, Alyse."

Ben dropped to the floor next to Anna and helped himself to an apple slice. "What files?"

"I recorded the last couple days. Ryan doesn't think the recording is accurate." I looked to Anna. "He doesn't think those things actually happened." Understanding dawned on her face so quickly I began to regain faith in my faculties.

"So then...he thinks something is wrong with your...*gear?*" she asked.

I saw her watching Ben and Ryan very carefully. After all, if those recordings were accurate, they would show her transforming into a black-eyed monster and doing her level-best to kill me. Attempted murder sort of trumped coercion.

When neither Ben nor Ryan showed any kind of reaction, she turned a questioning look at me. I shook my head ever so slightly.

As far as I knew Ryan had had no time to get that far back in the files. Her secret was safe.

"Ryan, might I have a word?"

To my surprise, Ben didn't protest. In fact, he dropped into Ryan's vacated spot next to Anna so fast, I couldn't keep my eyebrow from raising. I fought the urge to remind him what a certain Steffi Marisova would do to a certain antique Corvette named Monique, if he ever mentioned Anna's name more than once when he got home. I looked from him to Anna, just in time to see that tentative light flare to its full glory—her eyes, the way they should have been: glowing with a quiet, radiant joy. And I knew that my friend had worked for hours to put that there.

With a sigh, I turned away to lead Ryan out into the hall. We walked in the direction of the church, the rest of the barracks/ monastery having rather suspect flooring. In silence, we navigated the functional portions of the stairs. On that first landing, I crouched down and led the way through the miniature tunnel in the wall to the Church of the Gesuiti.

On the other side, I scooted out of the way and hunkered down in the small balcony, brushing crumbs of brick and stone from my knees. Ryan was broader through the shoulders than I. He had a few choice words to say as he pulled himself free of the decrepit stonework.

When he made it to his feet, Ryan paused for a moment as he took in the vastness of the space, carved up as it was by looters.

"Kills you to see what the world lost here. Just freakin' kills you."

"Yeah," I agreed quietly.

I waited until he had settled down, the sound of his boots scraping stone across stone echoing through the chamber startlingly loud. I kept my face forward.

"Tell me she knew something, Ryan."

"I'm sorry, Alyse. Near as I can tell, she just didn't want you near Matteo until he gets his meds straightened back out."

I squeezed my eyes shut in denial.

I'd gambled.

And I'd lost.

"They'll know I'm not dead. I've got a day. Maybe two."

"She won't tell."

I just shook my head. "She said it herself: she won't have to. You guys have to get out of here before that happens."

"I can't leave until I have something I can take to Booth."

I opened my eyes and turned to him. For a moment I hesitated, he wore the face that matched that voice from last night: the soldier's face. For a moment I didn't know him. I had to pretend I didn't see it just to get myself to speak.

"Look...we can be pretty sure this didn't happen before we got here. As much as we travel, Lone Pine Pictures doesn't have enough resources to hide that many kids."

Oh, yeah, what about those symptoms Jürgen taunted you with: the overpowering homesickness, the freakish aversion to touch? I ignored my own doubts and pressed on.

"So as long as Tamsin doesn't come back with some absolute wildcard, however this happened, it happened here and not because of a bunch of Sleeper DNA floating around the black market. It's contained—just like they always promised us it was."

"So just seal the city back up. Wi—with you in it." Ryan pressed his lips together over his broken words and stared fixedly at the remains of the pulpit across from us. It occurred to me that now he would have two people imprisoned by this disease: Haylee in the Children's Castle and me here in Venice with the monsters. There was one difference between Haylee and me, though. I picked up a red crumb of bloated brick and rolled it between my fingers until it had all fallen to dust.

"Eventually we'll all...we'll all be gone. And then it can never happen again."

"Alyse—"

"It can't take too much longer."

"Alyse."

"Ryan, there are *not* two hundred and thirty-eight people in this camp."

He froze. I tried to smile grimly, but the tremor in my hands came back to life and found its way to my face, twisting my expression.

"Please," I whispered, "you have to take Ben and you have to get yourself out of here."

But he just sat there and shook his goddamn head!

"You said one or two more days. We'll take every second we can get. Alyse, somebody's responsible. The barriers around this camp are not impenetrable. We have to find out who it is and we have to stop them."

That edgy, painful rattle of frustration and grief tearing at my solar plexus finally exploded. It threw me to my feet with a bitter snarl.

"Then you are going to goddamn die with me!"

Debris pelted the murky water as I vaulted the railing and conceded the field, taking my self-disgust with me. Why, just once, could I not muster the eloquence to make him understand?

Just this once when it actually mattered.

Chapter 6

That night it began.

It was as if the shadows created her from a touch of moonlight. From my perch on the windowsill, I hugged my knees and watched as the silver-blue shimmer of her dress slowly materialized, the iridescent fabric emerging from darkness, dancing on the ever present ocean breeze that wove through it like another layer of living silk.

Tendrils of silvery hair lifted and glided around that knowing smile as she came toward me, leaving the shadows' soft embrace. Then came those pale blue eyes, glittering with moonlight, with wicked amusement.

I rose to block her way.

I should have known better than to stand so close.

She raised a hand to my face, ran an ephemeral thumb across my cheekbone.

"Ah, my little Alyse! You did give our Hadria such a lovely hunt! She will be so bitterly disappointed to find you resurrected."

I reared my head to free myself from her grasp. Her gaze drifted past me to where Ryan slept. She giggled and the delighted chime of it drilled ice into the core of my forearms.

"Cirena," I warned.

"Be calmed, child," she murmured far too close to my ear. My breathing went shallow as I felt her watching my friend sleep. My hair tie snapped against the back of my head and the satin of my hair bloomed around my face, caught in Cirena's dancing sea breeze. She seized a lock of it around one of her delicate fingers. I froze, erasing the urge to yank it away from her. I had seen Cirena pissed; I knew what lay beneath this childish giddiness.

"I did not come to play with your sweet toys, young one."

"They are NOT toys!"

She caught my wrist before I could smack her hand away.

Shit!

Cirena kept me locked by the wrist as she tipped her head back and drew in a deep, satisfied breath. "Mmmm. I do see why Damon is so taken with you."

When she lowered her head, her eyes had changed. No longer glittering with moonlight, they *were* moonlight, cold, depthless, primal. I couldn't stop the tremor that crept through my shoulders. Somehow I knew I had just revealed something I really shouldn't have.

She drew me forward with that delicate steel grip. I used my grudging step on the slick roof tiles to more fully block the window.

"What would you do? Waste your boon and wish me away from those lovely little playthings?"

My boon for sparing her Anna. Not a chance in hell I was stepping into her twisted world by accepting her offer to dance. Not a chance in hell.

"What do you want, Cirena?"

"You misunderstand me, young one. I've simply come to bring you a gift."

Simply. Dr. Roz's warning about the covenant of indebtedness rang in my mind. There were no "simple" gifts here.

The fingers that held my hair released. Next to my cheek something glittered. Cautiously, I shifted my gaze from her face. A small drawstring bag dangled from her fingertips. Now it was my turn to draw a deep breath as the rich minerals of loamy earth filled my senses. I smelled the tang of evergreen leaves and that fresh, bright, almost cucumbery fragrance of cut wild grasses. I took the bag and pressed the rough-spun fabric to my nose, drinking down those scents like the smoothest whiskey, feeling the warmth flow into my core and slowly seep into my frozen extremities.

Cirena's voice caressed the edges of my glowing awareness.

"A gift and a message, young one. The one who sought to save your soul, the one who so foolishly, so very foolishly fought for you, he languishes in the prison of that hospital. Your beautiful Matteo, soon he will be forced to sacrifice yet another piece of his humanity to the Huntress. For serving as your protector...he...will...fall."

The last rush of her breath brushed across my cheek. Reluctantly, I drew the small, fragrant bundle from my face, my heart losing a little of that glow as it sank slowly into the sludge of guilt pooling at the center of my stomach.

"Matteo?" I whispered.

But Cirena was already stepping backward into her shadows, gathering them around her, filament by filament until they shrouded all but her voice.

"Will you save him?"

ॐ

I awoke the next morning to the sound of the rain. It fell in a steady, comforting rush on the roof tiles outside the window. I savored the cocoon of peace and vivid wakefulness just for a moment. I could scent my woods in that rich, healing water.

My woods, a half a world away.

I opened my eyes.

Clutched in my hand, centimeters from my face lay the little sachet. Cirena's sachet. I groaned.

"What is that smell?!"

Ben's cry of disgust came from another room. I heard a loud clatter and jumped to my feet. I had a bad feeling I knew exactly who that smell was.

As I came around the corner, Luciana batted at her tattered rags in an awkward attempt to put out the smoldering cloth which she had apparently dipped into one of our precious space heaters. I forced the breath from my chest. Luciana dry was pungent. Luciana soaked through...oh, lord, there were no words.

"Luciana, do...do you need help?"

My eyes seeped and my face burned by the time she managed to get the small cluster of embers smothered using the moisture from her own clothes.

"Demon fire, demon fire, demon fire!" she shrieked, jumping rhythmically away from the space heater like some sort of tribal dancer.

Skirting around, I righted the offending appliance before it lit up much more than her collection of ancient, shredded cloth. From that cocoon of warmth, I watched, waited until she had wound herself down from her frenzy. She huddled herself beneath the corner of windowsill in the long shadows of morning.

"Luciana, how did you find me?"

Abruptly, her head turned toward me.

"Our city, our sweet city, she knows where her souls lie, every last one, every last one."

Well, that was a Luciana answer.

I scraped at my watering eyes and held Cirena's sachet close to my face in the vain hope of blocking the smell. Though I could only make out the barest gleam of Luciana's eyes, I could sense her focus shift to that sachet. Slowly, she rose in the half light. From my crouch behind the heater, Luciana was much, much taller than I remembered.

A flutter of rags lifted from her side, a crone's gnarled finger pointed at the little bag clutched in my hand.

"Too late, too late! Already she lures you."

Abruptly, she crumpled up and skittered toward me. An arm's length away she stopped stock still.

"Do you ride with the mad moon? What did she offer you for your soul?" She cocked her hidden head. "Eyes black, black as the grave of the lagoon. Soul drained away. All hers. What did she offer you, little lost girl? What have you lost?"

Everything.

"Nothing, Luciana. I didn't, she just told me..." *Your beautiful Matteo, soon he will be forced to sacrifice yet another piece of his humanity to the Huntress. For serving as your protector...he...will...fall.*

"Mmmm," she hummed as she swayed back and forth before me, sending my eyes blurring once more. "Our sweet little Matti. You cannot save him. He wanders too far into the darkness, too far, too far."

A panic roiled in the acid emptiness of my stomach. Lost? Completely lost? And was that the gradual, inevitable fate of Anna, of me, of all the rest? Because just as clearly as I could remember the terror of his attack, I could also remember the gentle kindness of his company, the steady, determination of his defense against Cirena.

Next door I heard the shift and groan of Ben's great weight rising. The time to trade in secrets neared an end. Pinning my faceless oracle with a stare, I slid the heater aside and closed the crouched distance between us, scrapping up bundles of grey, frayed floorboard before my training shoes.

"Did he have a choice, Luciana? How...how can he be damned for choices he didn't make, didn't know he was making?"

"Alyse? What—?" Ben's steps stopped at a distance, mostly likely the doorframe. "Uff! I shoulda known."

Unwilling to lose this chance, I forced myself closer, though the chemistry of her foul defenses pressed me physically back.

"Luciana, how?"

Those tatters folded inward. A cloud of herb-scented exhalation momentarily cleared the burn from my face. Luciana's shrieking lilt fell to a murmur.

"He gave himself, our Matti, gave himself as prey...."

Before I could coax myself to breathe, Luciana skittered to the windowsill. With one hand on the stone, she twisted back.

"*To give oneself as a prey to many, with the risk of being deprived, robbed, and killed, of being able to lose in only one day what you had earned over a long time, with so many dangers of injuring yourself, of catching contagious and terrifying diseases; to eat with someone else's mouth, to sleep with someone else's eyes, to move according to someone else's desires, clearly running toward the wreckage of your faculties and your life; what misery could be worse?*"

"Nothing." That was Anna.

"Listen to the girl, lost and wary Alyse. This is what you risk if you fall for the shadow woman's deceit, for the moonlight's lure. He falls into the abyss for you, little Matti, little Matti, to *a perdition and certainty of damnation*. For you. Leave him, leave to him his honor."

In a puff of dust, she spun back toward the window and bounded out into the gray sunlight of morning.

More slowly I rose and turned to face my audience. Ryan stood propped against the doorframe on my left, carefully avoiding the protruding nails. Ben stood with Anna in the opposing doorway, carefully avoiding my gaze. Manners forced my eyes away from the halo of tangles rising from the back of Anna's blonde head.

"So they know we're here already."

I nodded to Ryan, pressing my sachet to my face. God, if I didn't get a shower soon, *I* was going to start smelling like that!

"We got our first visitor last night: Cirena," I told him. Out of the corner of my eye, I saw Anna pale ever so slightly. I understood then that I'd likely done her no favors when I'd delivered her to her mistress the other night on the palace step. A lifetime ago.

"So dude, who is little Matti, little Matti? And what's the deal about him goin' to hell for you? And you should just let him? That chick is so freaked!" Ben shook his head out, rubbed at his face with the scrape of morning stubble.

"Matteo Ranier," Ryan answered for me.

"That dude you danced with at the party?"

They all walked into the room now to crouch nearer to the space heater and I lowered myself to the floor with them. Anna caught me staring at her hair. She discreetly reached a hand up and tried to comb it down. I still couldn't process that Ben had knowingly sacrificed Monique the Corvette to Steffi's rage. Because she would find out. Psycho Steffi always found out. If he even shared drinks with a girl, she found out.

Monique for a one night stand with a carrier? What the hell?

Ben snapped his fingers in front of my face. I jerked my attention over to him. "Alyse, why is he going to hell? For dancing with you? For doing the deed with you? What's this leave him his honor crap?"

A carefully blank spot in my memory panicked at the threat of his questions. Anna and I looked to one another and her hand slowly left off tending her hair.

"He will be re-entered into the treatment program. This afternoon, I think," Anna replied carefully. I raised an eyebrow. Cirena had said he was already there.

Ryan searched my face, then hers.

"Why? What does this have to do with *perdition and damnation*?"

"Some of us believe that the treatments slowly peel away our humanity. Luciana thinks we are selling off pieces of our souls to the devil to free ourselves from earthly torment."

Ben leaned back on his heels and dropped to his butt, wrapped his arms around his jeans-clad knees. "Whoa, did I mention that chick was freaked?"

Except from what I'd seen, she really wasn't. *To eat with someone else's mouth, to sleep with someone else's eyes, to move according to someone else's desires, clearly running toward the wreckage of your faculties and your life...* To let Hadria overtake you utterly... That was the *perdition and damnation* Matteo was headed for.

"But that doesn't answer why." Ryan was nothing if not persistent.

Now it was Anna's turn to silently push me to answer.

"He...." I took a breath and started over. "He tried to stop them. He tried to protect me."

Anna's shoulders dropped and she gave me a hard look. "Maybe, but that's not why he's being sent back into the treatment program."

They all stared at me, waiting. That tremor threatened again, in my chest, in my stomach, in my arms and the legs I tucked carefully underneath me. I was tired of it. This was not me. This was not who I was going to be. I lowered the sachet from my face, rested my hands on my knees and waited. I waited until the steady rush of the sea beyond the shattered window behind me overtook the rattling discord in my nerves, until it soothed the crawling fire in my veins. I waited for my shark god's peace and hope to settle into my chest once more.

"Alyse, baby, what exactly happened that night?"

I raised my eyes to see Ben's eyebrows pinched together with both worry and fear—and a little touch of guilt.

"Matteo, he's the one who attacked me."

"What?! A busted arm, three busted ribs? I'll bust his goddamn pretty-boy face! Accident, my ass!" Ben surged to his feet hard enough to splinter a floorboard under his boot. I rose more quietly.

"Ben, the thing is, he didn't know what he was doing. Almost like it wasn't him doing it at all."

Ben whipped around, drove a finger at my face.

"Do NOT make excuses for that dead shit! If he busted you up that bad, he coulda killed you. No battalion of lil' 'bots gonna fix that, no matter how many of those goddamn pills you choke down!"

I could just see the edge of Anna's shirt rise up behind him. She stepped around him and laid a hand on his arm.

"She's right, Ben. He probably didn't know what he was doing."

He turned on her. "Don't you start, too."

"Ben," I warned. Amazingly, though, Anna didn't back down. If anything, she glowed even brighter with that serenity I'd wished for her, seen in her just the day before. Ben's stance softened. He lowered his finger.

"Alright, then you gonna tell me this: how could a guy NOT know he was beatin' a girl, a strong girl with a shitload of training, how could he NOT know he was beatin' her to death?"

I stepped around Ryan and the space heater so I could get a better look at Anna's face when I answered. "They told me someone had messed with his meds. Is that true? Or was it more like..." ...*like what Hadria did to you when she forced you to hunt?*

Anna gave a small shake of her head to reply to my unspoken question. Not Hadria... Distracted by the new hole in my understanding, I nodded and sank back down to the floor next to Ryan. Anna pulled Ben back to sitting as well.

Anna continued. "That's more of a party line. A euphemism, I guess, might be a better word. It's not that simple. But with all our precautions, it should never have happened. I don't know what they've found out. But I do know...." She sighed and that glow flickered for just a brief second. "I do know that Matteo is a good guy and this, this might be more than he can take. Just too much, you know?"

I did know. I remembered the face of the Asian guy at the end of the hall—that wrecked hopelessness. I closed my eyes and sighed. The scent of Matteo returned to me, the smell of his jacket on my shoulders, the rich, warm glide of his hands across my skin. He could touch me.

He could touch me.

God.

"Sounds like a bunch a bullshit to me," Ben grumbled.

I smiled grimly and opened my eyes. "I wish it was."

Ryan moved for the first time. He crossed his legs and sat up to look straight at me. "So this Cirena, was it? She is trying to bait you into rescuing Matteo. This other...person," he waved toward the window, "is warning you not to."

"Luciana," I supplied.

"Luciana," he repeated. "But it's Phan Mai that has him. Cirena works with Phan Mai?"

"No, no, absolutely not," Anna murmured, shaking her head. "Cirena, I have a feeling, is trying to get the pawns back into play." She looked up at me. "You can't capture what isn't on the board."

And I was one of those pawns. I fingered the gift of a tear-shaped pendant that hung between my breasts. Cirena would use Matteo, would use Ben and Ryan to force me into position. And so would Jürgen Phan Mai.

"Jürgen. We only have hours, maybe minutes until he finds out Anna's gone and figures out I'm not dead. Until he finds out you two are here with me."

"Alyse—"

"Ryan, that was our deal. Once you were on the radar, you were out of here. You'll just have to trust me to be your eyes and hands until—"

"We're going in after him." I froze and stared. Ryan pushed to his feet. "We'll go now before Phan Mai has time to get ready. You said Matteo was one of the inner circle. He's vulnerable, headed toward hell your Luciana said. Probably mentally already in hell, if what Anna says is true. He'll talk."

I looked at Ryan's eyes with their half-lowered lids, his lips drawn into a thin line. Why did I feel a sudden need to protect Matteo from one of my best friends? Matteo, who was offering up his soul for me. Matteo, who'd had his head fucked with by...someone. Someone who was not Hadria. Could we have the same ass to kick? For a second I closed my hand around his pendant on its filament chain, then dropped it back beneath the shelter of my winter-weave shirt.

Ryan saw the expression on my face change and I hesitated, knowing what my priority had to be.

"And then you'll keep your promise?" I demanded.

Ryan gave a sharp nod. I looked over to Ben. He had taken Anna's hand in his. No more Steffi, then. Never liked her anyway, I reminded myself. Still...

This time I was the one to jump to my feet.

"She stays. She will never be able to keep up."

Chapter 7

I was acting like that jackass, Vittorio.

I perched in the jagged maw of yet another palace, dusted the shimmer of ancient glass crumbs from my gloves. Framed by the shattered teeth of what once must have been the graceful tipped arches of four stone-framed windows, I looked out over yet another flooded alleyway.

The endless, menacing labyrinth that was Venice.

Mo, I need to calm down. I've got to calm down. I'm going to screw up everything.

Perhaps medications remain here in the treatment center.

What?!

Here in the mental health treatment center.

Very funny.

Trust the Venetians to house their crazies in a palace.

I took a deep breath, listened to Anna yelp, followed shortly by Ben's muted curse. Even Ryan's breathing was audible from somewhere below. I was running them brutally hard. And yet I could barely keep a leash on my need to barrel onward. I wanted what lay on the other end of this journey: smash, grab, and then the boys gone. I had failed once with Anna. I would not, could not fail again.

My heart thudded against my sternum, giving lie to my careful logic.

Mo, I need to calm down.

I craned my neck past the remains of flower boxes and looked up. Looters had surgically removed a huge chunk from the face of the palace, leaving sections of the upper floor to collapse.

What could have been so valuable about the sign on an insane asylum that they had to tear down half the building to haul it off?

It was not the sign for the facility. It was a statue of Chronos, god of time, with the very sun cradled in his hands. "Finché girerà questo sole, Zara, Cattaro, Capodistria, Verona, Cipro, Creta, culla di Giove, faranno testimonianza delle mie azioni."

She translated, *For as long as the sun shall rise, Zadar, Kotor, Koper, Verona, Cyprus, and Crete, the very birthplace of Zeus, shall bear testimony to my actions.*

Whose actions?

The great statesman and scholar, Gianmatteo Bembo. This was his home, Palazzo Bembo-Boldú. The shell of St. James below the Chronos statue would have symbolized his study of alchemy.

He was a sorcerer? I thought you said scholar.

Alchemy was the precursor to modern chemistry. The sea shell represented St. James, the patron saint of alchemists and physicians—those who sought to free nature and man from their flawed temporal existence and elevate them to immortal perfection.

A sudden and jarring image of Dr. Frankenstein's monster flashed through my head. Nothing good ever came of messing with humans' flawed temporal existences. Dr. Franco had tried to mess with the Brighton's patients' flawed temporal existences.

And here we were.

Or maybe Captaini Bembo simply had a preference for sea shells.

I chuckled. *Maybe.*

I clung to the half-smile Mo had gifted me and immersed myself in it, let it smooth away some of my jittery fear and anger. I took another look up at the path I'd taken to Anna's grocery last time.

Not happening.

A small, soft, and torn hand groped the masonry at my feet and I pulled my trainer-clad foot from the sill.

Definitely not happening.

I crouched down, grasped her around the wrist, and heaved. Anna got her waist over the ledge. With my help and a shove from Ben, she tumbled the rest of the way over.

"A little different coming up than going down?"

She nodded and used her sleeve to wipe the sweat from her face as she scrambled out of the way to let Ben over. Rock chips and mortar sprayed everywhere as Ben's belt buckle took out a chunk of the ledge when he came up behind her. Ryan popped up next, wearing the dusting of glass and stone caked on his sweat-soaked face. He made it over the edge and spit a mouth full of it back over the side.

"Thanks, man. Really."

"Don't mention it." Ben dropped his head back against the partial brick wall behind him and closed his eyes. "How much further?"

"About two or three more blocks," I replied.

"And we've come how far?"

"About four."

"Shiiiit."

"And that's just 'till we get to Anna's. The palace is twice this far." I glanced over to Anna and we shared a twisted little smile. Dropping into a squat, I swung off my daypack and dug out a water bottle for Ryan who had sprawled against the crumpled wall without any regard for his precious case of swarm cameras. I tossed it at him. He actually managed to catch it.

I rose and stretched at the muscles in my limbs that I knew I needed to maintain carefully if I was going to have any energy left for the smash and grab at the end of this little adventure.

With a sigh, I glanced upward.

"Rest here for a sec. I'm going to have to find us a different path back to Anna's campo. We need to pick up the pace."

"Pick up the pace? Pick UP the pace?" Ben demanded.

"Yeah, and don't get too comfortable. Your muscles will start seizing up."

"Uh, hello, trainer here," he reminded me.

I kicked him in the foot. "Coulda fooled me. Be right back."

Honestly, I didn't know how we'd made it this far without getting a little call from our favorite overlord. The clouds worked in our favor, blinding his eyes in orbit, but there were other ways to find people and I had no doubt Jürgen had access to those technologies.

Maybe word truly hadn't reached him. I suspected he breathed rather rarified air, even here.

I stepped over Anna's legs and headed down the hall. Except for the damage done by looters, this palazzo was fairly well preserved, being protected from the direct anger of an abused Adriatic by several blocks worth of neighbors. I found the first hall and turned down it.

Keep me pointed in the right direction, Mo. We don't have time—or energy—to waste here.

Acknowledged.

I walked across a fallen door and peered into a room. The cave-in from the upper level had decimated the floor, but we were just two layers from the roof which had not collapsed. Carefully, I trotted down the hall. If I could use the rubble to get them to the roof, we could make much better time. These buildings were practically stacked on top of one another. I ducked into the next room. Solid floor, much less collapse damage.

I clambered up the chunks of wall with an eye trained on the splintered wood construction above me.

"You know how much danger they will be in."

Startled, I missed my grip on the beam I'd aimed for. My feet went sliding. I just barely managed to grab the edge of an alcove behind me before my ass could go next.

Seeing Anna in the doorway, I took a second to breathe through the lash of anger. I lowered myself to sitting. She stepped inside the room and I recognized the fairness in her lack of apology. Her gaze never left mine, watching, weighing the effect of each word.

"Luciana isn't entirely wrong. Especially about the ones she calls *fate*. They don't perceive humanity the same way we do. Jürgen and Suzi are so close to the edge of it. Sometimes it is like you can see their souls flicker in and out of existence right in front of you."

I gave my head a small tilt, but otherwise held myself still, leaving the air open for her to continue.

"Luciana told me a story once—while she was busy stealing my dinner. She said the sultan in Constantinople had requested a painter from Venice, a cultural exchange. At one point the sultan requested the scene of Salome dancing with St. John the Baptist's head. You know that story, I'm sure."

Anna wandered further into the room and her steady gaze turned from me. Somewhere at the edge of my awareness awoke the dark press of menace. We had circled each other in an abandoned room once before. I kept to my place, kept my peace. But I watched the way she moved, down to the flutter of her fingers as she brushed back her hair.

"The sultan loved the painter's work, Bellini Gentle, Gentile, something like that, but he said to him, 'the neck sticks out too far, when a man is decapitated, the neck retracts.' Bellini begged to differ. The sultan, well, he, he called for a slave, Alyse, and he had the guards chop the guy's head off. Just like that. Just so he could show Bellini what he meant."

Anna turned back to me then, her eyes a shocking, pleading blue.

"Do you understand, Alyse? You and I, they will play in their power struggle, but Ben, Ryan...."

Her quiet voice shushed into the silence. For a moment, I looked away, watched the dust dance in a dim ray from the broken stories above. I'd seen that flicker, felt that inhuman aura, knew the threat. My own voice was quiet when I replied with a short laugh.

"What do you suggest? I take a two-by-four to the pair of them? Ryan has a niece in a Children's Castle, Anna. That's what it would take."

For a minute I thought of Haylee with her soft brown hair arranged so neatly on the pillow, thought of the permitted pair I would never have. What would they have looked like cuddled sleepily on my lap before bedtime, climbing the furniture in death-defying acts of grinning obliviousness? How might they have felt growing inside me, little kicks and punches, rolls and turns? What a sensory file that would have been!

And what I would have gone through to keep them safe, my own permitted pair. My whole body tightened, trying to wrap around these imaginary children of mine. Ryan had stood by Haylee for ten years. It would take more than a two-by-four. It would take answers.

As if she had watched my daydream with me, I raised my head to see tears dancing at the edge of her lids.

"My babies," she whispered. "Sixteen of them. I read them a story as they curled up for nap time. Bertie and the Butterfly Dance. They never woke up. Their parents came... Can Ryan really do someth—but Dr. Franco, ten years, Alyse, and he's got nothing."

I rose from the rocks that had caught me and walked to her. I gave her shoulder a firm squeeze, carefully avoiding the edges of her floral blouse purely out of habit.

"He can't wake your babies up, Anna. He can't wake up Haylee. But he can keep this from happening to anybody else's baby. *We* can keep this from happening to anybody else's baby."

Over her shoulder, I nodded to the boys.

Anna turned, but stayed at my side. "I have a boat, a couple boats. I can guide you. Once you have him, I can take you someplace you can talk. But you will have to be fast, ask him what you need to know and get out. You cannot begin to imagine how powerful Jürgen truly is until you have made an enemy of him."

Ryan nodded. "Understood."

My Grocery Girl of soft flowers and swaying grasses led the way up the tumble of masonry. And if her movements were too fluid, her strength just a little more than natural, her eyes remained a burning, relentless blue.

Chapter 8

I knew Anna had no AI, but nonetheless, her orientation in this maze of tumbled hallways and dammed canals proved faultless. Because her shop was closed, the foot traffic in the campo consisted of a construction worker and the same coffee drinker as before. Within minutes we darted in tight formation across the alley and entered the shop by a most unconventional means: the front door.

Anna led the way through the short window aisle and unlocked a large closet near the door. There stood the yellow kayak. Next to it, a shallow aluminum fishing boat tricked out for hauling flats of groceries.

"The problem will be getting these to the water. When you've lived with the same two hundred people for ten years, strangers really catch the eye. That and the next delivery isn't due until Saturday."

Ben reached in and hefted the aluminum boat. It rose easily, but his hand still shook from all the climbing. I knew we were all in the same shape. I shared a glance with Ryan. He was thinking the same thing.

"I know we are chasing the clock, but I think we need to take ten, rest and eat—especially if you are right about how fast we'll need to move once we get to the palace." He pulled one strap of his daypack off his shoulder and nodded at Ben to put the boat down. "Anna, do you have a map we could take a look at together?"

"Upstairs?" I suggested.

Ben closed the closet and jerked his head toward the display windows.

"Unless you go and hire them manikin people on a regular basis." He picked up a box of crackers and cocked his head at an artificial angle as he gestured to it.

Anna laughed and that hard edge fell away from her. I wasn't sure we were done needing superhuman Anna quite yet, but I kept my mouth shut as I followed them up the side stairs to the storage area. As the boys and I cleared a workspace on the top of a crate of cereal, she pulled a clipboard down from a nail near the window over the kitchen sink. Leafing through it, she tugged an old tourist map free. It had been heavily edited to reflect those Venetian "paths" and other modifications wrought by time and neglect. Somewhere a museum curator was groaning in mortification. Anna smoothed it carefully over the cereal boxes.

"We're here at the Campo Santa Marina. There are two points where we can enter the cleared waterways: diagonal across the campo here next to the Palazzo Marcello or here where the bridge used to be by the Palazzo Bragadin Carraba. Marcello is less public, but I think the construction crews are using it. With the bigger boat, we are going to have to head for the Grand Canal. You'll have to follow me exactly. There's a lot of submerged debris that can rip the bottom out of a boat."

That I remembered clearly.

Ben's fingers moved through the air, making notes on his own map.

Mo, why don't you file that map, too. We're probably going to need it, seeing as we'll be staying a while.

Done.

Ryan traced the Grand Canal with a finger. "Not very secluded."

"Most of us live here in the campo or at the palace. The canal and the other sea-facing properties get hit too hard by the storms. Too unstable. That aquarium glass is the only reason the palace is even habitable."

I frowned, remembering the chase down that waterway. "But you guys don't stay in the campo or the palace all the time and that is a really big stretch of open water."

"Yeah, say somebody's out stretching their legs."

Anna smiled gently over at Ben. "You would call what we've been doing for the last hour 'stretching your legs'? And the brickwork is even more rotten along the canal."

Incoming call from Tamsin Leonides.

I hesitated. But maybe she'd found something. Maybe we could skip the sloppiest raid ever planned.

I'll take it.

I stepped back from the group, settled against a wall, and closed my eyes. Tamsin's avatar sprang to life in my mind's eye—hot pink leggings, flowing white blouse, and long layers of glittering rose beads. Another life, another world.

"I've got it! I've got it! Oh, my god, Alyse honey, you will not believe how hard my heart's racing right now!" She flopped dramatically against the gunmetal grey wall of our online meeting room. I narrowed my eyes.

"What have you got, Tamsin?"

She held up a holographic data cube. "All of it. Her entire system."

I felt myself blanch both on and offline.

"Tamsin, those are medical records! You could go to federal prison!"

"Oh, don't be such a ninny, 'Lyse! I won't snoop. I didn't have time to sort through it. Her apartment is next door to the complex! I bought a system to process your DNA chart, but you need to send me a copy of your dog tag."

Ninny? Now we really were channeling 1930's girl detectives.

"Fine. Mo is sending it now. I've got to go. I might be offline for a few hours, but let me know what you find out as soon as you can."

Tamsin popped back up off the wall. "Sure thing! Oh, your mom said to call when you have a minute."

Midway to logging off, I paused. "How is she doing, Tamsin?"

"Oh, good. She's been out hiking with Emory a couple times. Hooked up with that renter gal from your old place."

"She shouldn't miss the bonfire. She would love Sebastian."

I'd been going to take her to the bonfire. I sighed, trying to let go of a life that was simply no longer mine.

Tamsin laughed. "Everybody loves Sebastian. It's those arms, honey. Okay and all that glorious hair. Hmm, maybe those wicked eyes."

"I meant his storytelling, Tamsin," I said wryly.

"Oh, absolutely, that voice turns me into a lil ol' puddle of hormones every time."

"When you're done with that little fantasy, tell Mom I will call her." Because lying to my mother's face was so very high on my to-do list.

God.

Tamsin quieted, her face softening. "Yeah, 'Lyse. I will. Take care of our boys, ya hear?"

I scraped the escaped tendrils back from my face as I nodded.

"I'm trying. Seems like the harder I try, the less it works."

Tamsin chuckled softly. "Now you know how I've felt all these years."

"I suppose I do."

And this time when I smiled at her, I meant it.

୭

"Who was it?"

I blinked back to reality and looked up at Ryan. Two things I noticed: the first, his entire body radiated a coiled energy about ready to burst – it was time to go; the second, sunlight. My head jerked to the window and I scrambled up.

"It was Tamsin. I was hoping she found something to make this little errand unnecessary. No such luck." I looked up at the crack of sky between buildings. It could go either way, but there were definitely breaks in those black clouds, breaks Jürgen could see through.

"What did she say?"

"She downloaded the doc's ENTIRE system." Ryan's eyes grew wide and Ben stopped to turn from Anna back to us. "She's going to compare the DNA chart against my dog tag herself. She's developing some sort of Nancy Drew complex. Anyway, she'll get back to us. But this sun, this is not good. We gotta get out of here. I assume you three hatched a plan for getting the boats launched?"

"Yep. You and me hop out this window and scout out the alley and the dock. Give Anna and Ben the all clear."

Again, with the fucking window.

"The door broken?"

"Lunch crowd of two settling in next door. Two legs sticking out from behind a boat, maybe. Six, not so much."

I had to concede the point. He slapped a peeled hard-boiled egg in my hand, held up a bag of carrots, slipped a chocolate bar and a water bottle into the holster on my daypack. I took a huge bite of the egg and stuffed the carrots into a pocket in my cargoes. A far cry from my favorite Tom Kah Gah soup back home, but anything real tasted amazing after three days of peanut butter-flavored chemicals.

Ryan shoved open the old window and a gust of barely forgotten fall air burst into the room. I turned back to Ben and Anna.

Whoops.

My own neglected hormones set the roots of my hair on fire as I caught Ben inhaling Anna face-first.

O-kaaaay.

Ryan and I shared an awkward split-second glance.

Steffi who?

"I'll go," I mumbled, then stuffed the other half of the egg in my mouth and spun my lower half out the window, flipped over, and scooted down to a dangle. At that point, I remembered the rope in my pack and cursed my hasty evacuation. I let myself drop. For the barest moment my toes made contact with the edge of the flower box beneath me; I begged it to hold as I shoved myself out and back toward the cobblestone. Blinking, I held my breath as my shins took my name in vain jarringly, repeatedly.

I reached up and Ryan tossed me his precious pack. I glanced down the alley. Still clear.

Ryan was short. I dropped his pack against the wall and got behind him as he swung over the window sill. He managed through sheer hand strength to transfer himself from a fingertip hold on the upper sill to a fingertip hold on the top of the lower sill, using his trainers wedged against the sides of the frame for traction and balance. His feet met the bottom sill. He twisted to jump. I threw my hands up.

"Watch the flower—"

The best I could do was deflect the energy of his fall. I swung as much of his weight past me as I could. He did a fair job of rolling through it, but he scrambled to his feet limping in the middle of the wide alleyway, exposed to the increasing daylight.

We both looked around frantically for an audience.

The voices from around the corner echoed startlingly loud across the stone. A power drill started up.

Ryan darted forward to grab his gear. I led the way at a sprint toward the safety and shadows of the narrower alley next to the palace. Only in the darkness did I risk a glance over my shoulder.

"Ankle?"

"Nothin'."

He still limped, but not alarmingly. I turned back and stumbled to an abrupt halt.

The Asian businessman.

I threw my arm out to catch Ryan, nearly clotheslined him. I stepped between predator and prey. But that was the extent of my bravado. My chest tightened to the point of pain.

Breathe!

Did this guy just pace the damn alley like some kind of caged polar bear?!

The man just stood and stared at me. I could do little but stare back, force Ryan to take a short step of retreat. The alley was barely wide enough for two people to pass. Carefully, with pleading eyes I gestured Ryan back toward a doorway. The guy stalked us, just as Anna had done that first horrible night.

Ryan thought the biggest danger these carriers offered was Jürgen's threat against our families and those of the other gala attendees. What he didn't know just might get him out of here in one piece.

Let me lead him off. He's old and clumsy. I've outrun him before. Get to the dock. I'll meet you there.

I'll take him down. He's going to tell Phan Mai.

He's not a soldier, Ryan. Get out of here, now!

Deliberately, I raised a hand to ward off the man. He grabbed my wrist with a grip that was far too powerful.

"Go now!" I snarled at Ryan.

He looked startled as he slipped past me and the Asian and back into the street. I had a bad feeling my new disease was showing a little too clearly on my face. I heard his footsteps pounding away and knew Ben and Anna would come up behind him shortly.

I let the old man in the tired white business shirt push me further into the building and clear of the alley.

Okay, now what?

I tried to keep my focus on the carrier while I stole glances at the halls and doors around me. Abruptly, I found myself slammed back against the wall. My knuckles rapped the plaster as he pinned my arm back, dug his other set of fingers violently into my ribs.

"I don't want to!" he spit into my face.

Instinct pushed me to fight back, to punch and kick and tear into him with tooth and claw. One look at his face told me not to. I'd seen that look before.

I forced an artificial calm through my body. No predator. No prey.

"Then don't."

Something next to my head glowed a muted emerald. I risked a glance. This guy wore that same metal vambrace as Jürgen and Matteo hidden beneath his shirt. It glowed like it was about to detonate.

"You think..." He was panting now. "You think there's a choice? Haven't had a fucking choice about anything since the day I signed that goddamn form!"

My head slammed against the plaster a second time. My ribs screamed.

"What can I do?" I ignored the pain, tried to soothe him with my tone, my gentled eyes.

"Don't exist! Disappear! You destroyed everything! Our freedom! My freedom!" He punctuated his accusations by bashing my body against the wall. Obviously, I didn't have Anna's power to calm with a glance. "Years, I fought her for years! Now this!"

He released me to rip at the sleeve covering the neon emerald.

I didn't wait to admire the jewelry. I dropped to slam my forehead into his nose, came up again with an uppercut to his solar plexus. One thing about narrow, boney hands: they hurt more. He folded. I bolted down the hall.

I hadn't seen Anna and Ben go by with the boats yet. I needed to lead him away from the alley.

Oh, yeah, and not die trying.

Anna's map have anything about this building?

Uncertain. There are red scratch marks on this building.

Show me.

An image of Anna's map flashed into my mind's eye. I nearly ran right into a wall.

Shut it off! Shut it off!

Shit! I couldn't do both. I was on my own.

Behind me, I heard the Asian's shriek of frustrated anger, shift. The sound dropped to octaves he should never been able to reach, turned to a bellowing wildcat's roar. That roar began to climb, up, up a roar to a snarl, through a scream, then it broke apart into the two-tone cry of a hawk. My stomach heaved, every muscle in my body tried to lock up.

I grabbed a corner of the hallway and launched myself around it. Half the plaster came off under the force of my grip, ripping at my fingers. I heard the sound of his dress shoes beginning to pick up rhythm behind me.

To my right a pair of doors dangled against each other, holding up clumps of moss. I dropped to the muddy floor and slid through the triangle beneath them, careful not to bump them.

Are they there yet? I messaged Ryan.

Just came around the corner.

Get those boats in the water!

I slipped and slid to my feet, through the gravely muck. Plants. This was someone's shadowy greenhouse. I skirted a huge fern and saw light: a huge window at the other end of the room. Behind me I heard the predator's tapping skid to a halt. He saw my trail.

Move!

I jumped a flat of bleeding hearts, barely caught my footing on the other side. The doors slammed inward, shaking the tattered walls. The Asian grunted and roared in rage as they fell again.

Metal shrieked.

Pottery shattered.

I grabbed the smooth stone of the window's balcony.

"Now!"

Ryan looked up from setting the paddle on his kayak. Ben and Anna were already on the water. With shocking speed, he shot the little yellow boat into the canal.

I swung over.

The Asian caught a lock of my ponytail.

Hanging one armed, I yanked.

I dropped.

It wasn't the movies. The kayak rocked wildly. I lost enough hair to go blind with tears. Ryan somehow managed to catch the wall and strong-arm us into stability. Sightless, I found my seat behind him by instinct alone.

"Go!"

The monster, that monster would not follow us into the water.

I remembered that much.

But I still didn't want Ryan to see his eyes.

Chapter 9

I could not, however, silence the Asian's inhuman screams of rage. Ryan didn't dare twist around as we shot down the narrow canal behind the gleaming aluminum boat that held Ben and Anna, but I could see his alarm in his overly erect posture, in the jerk in his rowing rhythm.

I said nothing.

We took the corner, following Anna's placement exactly, and soon we were out in the relative wide-open of the Grand Canal. I released a rush of horded breath and tried to settle back in my seat.

The course of my nightmare run looked different in the shifting shadows and light of a stormy daytime. The quiet was almost peaceful once we escaped the ricochet of alarm cries.

I looked up at the wind-whipped clouds. As if bending to my will, the cracks in their formations began to seal. A spectacular autumn storm was on the horizon. I used my sleeve to clear the chill of tears from my face.

You okay?

Yeah.

Psycho seemed like he was trying to kill you.

He was pretty pissed.

Thought you said he was old and feeble.

I rubbed the spot on my head where that "geezer" had thinned my hair.

Maybe it's me who's getting old and feeble.

Ryan chuckled and shook his head.

Ben stopped darting looks at the towering ruins funneling us toward the Adriatic and craned around to spear us with a look.

"What's so funny?"

I froze in the midst of rebinding my hair in a ponytail and the grin slipped from my cheeks. His face was gray. Had he seen? Did he know? I tried to look past him to Anna. Did she still have control? She didn't glance back to confirm or deny.

"What's so funny?" Ryan shot back. "Your driving. That ain't no 'Vette, dude. Keep trying to corner like that and you're going to take the lady for a swim."

"More right!" Just over the rising wind I heard Anna mutter something about letting the lady do the driving and Ben turned away, put his attention back to the oars.

I pulled the last loop of hair through and lowered my hands to the side of the kayak. Even my most vicious grip on the fiberglass couldn't control the ripple of residual adrenaline.

I saw Ryan about to turn to me and I cut him off.

"So what's this then? Your neon yellow Aston Martin DB, Mr. Bond?"

"Nope, no ejection button for snarky passengers."

I laughed. "Never really had my eye on the role of Bond girl anyway."

"Still think you would have made an awesome Vesper."

"Are you kidding? She doesn't even kick any ass."

"She doesn't have to. She breaks him better than any of those other over-sexed chicks ever did."

I rolled my eyes. Ryan was squarely on Team Tamsin when it came to Bryce.

"Seriously? Are any of you ever going to let this go?"

"Dude, you didn't spend six months scraping him off the floor."

"Yeah, he was so heartbroken."

I watched the palazzo on our right float by dramatically in the shadows of the roiling clouds. The arcade, the rooftop, the gaping doorways and windows with their audiences of moss and sea grass watched me in return. Part of my mind surveyed the depths behind that audience for signs of movement, a vague concern for responses to the Asian's hunting call lurking in my own shadows. The rest of my soul drank in the banter while it was still mine. In our vagabond profession, we had made our home in each other. Beyond my forest and my little sachet of pine needles and woodland debris, my deepest restoration lay in the subtext of companionable sarcasm, in heated, meaningless debate of shoes, cars, spy gadgets, and stories. Tamsin. Ben. Ryan. And me.

And it was because they meant so much, that I would use that two-by-four if I had to. And it was because we meant so much, that I would probably have to.

"Alyse."

"Yeah?"

"That part was actually kinda true."

"What?"

"The six months part."

I straightened and pulled my attention away from those haunting shadows. Ryan was glancing back at me from the corner of his eye. I raised an eyebrow. He shrugged.

"Just thought you should know."

I let the confusion on my face answer for me. Ryan Gunner scraping Bryce Deacon off the floor for six months? I couldn't even build the picture in my mind. Bryce so broken he needed...

"Kinda promised him I wouldn't say anything, but now—" Ryan snapped forward to make an abrupt course adjustment. We rocked, then steadied as he straightened us out.

I didn't know.

Things got...sort of...well, pretty messed up between you two. Yeah.

Reality faded for a moment as a memory floated over me, Bryce's long narrow fingers running their own lines along my ribs, the long muscles of his torso, his legs pressed tight against mine, his hooded eyes burning azure like the sky behind him. I closed my eyes and released a weary sigh.

He keeps saying he can help me. He keeps saying not to believe anything these people tell me. I keep wondering what it is he thinks he knows.

Should probably give him a chance to tell you.

And abruptly that hypnotic memory flew apart, shattered by blows of rage and a scream of pain and fear. I snapped back to the moment, awkwardly dropped the hands that had risen in defense. Old, old memories. Old secrets.

Best left forgotten.

I could just see the Doge's Palace ahead of us, lights blazing in the dim afternoon.

Matteo.

Again, with the fucking shaking hands.

I jerked them out from between myself and Ryan and returned to gripping the boat. My leg muscles screamed to twitch against his after so long a confinement. I wanted up. I wanted out.

"Sure I can't take a turn with the rowing?"

"Not without beating me to death with the oar."

"Right."

"Don't worry, Vesper, there will be plenty of ass-kicking to attend to momentarily."

Not if any of the big boys got hold of us.

We swung out and around a sandbar built of someone's ruined palace.

Ca' Dario, the cursed palace.

Mo pulled up an image of an ornately decorated narrow palace with most of its face built of those tapered arch windows the Venetians were so fond of. Each layer was decorated with a distinctive circle, ringed with smaller circles carved of stone and surrounded with an almost gold rockwork. I just shook my head.

Not right now, Mo, but thanks.

Those lights were so close now.

I forced myself to relax.

The Palazzo Ducal. It was built to intimidate, built to show the might of the Venetian empire to anyone who might dare challenge her maritime power. Even with a full floor submerged, it towered devastatingly. Anna guided us forward, clinging to the shadow of the palace. I tried to suppress the anticipation of the slathering horde of feral carriers that had last followed me here.

Like the after-image of a dead relative in their own home after the funeral, I kept seeing them where they had been: on the pier, pouring over the arcade, scrabbling around the side of the palace from the blocked canal. The blocked canal that the grayed silver of Anna's grocery boat now turned into.

The shush of the sea remained uninterrupted.

It didn't stop my heart from drumming.

Then it was our turn.

Every muscle in my body tensed, ready to spring from the boat. I scooted back in my seat, shifted my grip on the boat.

That beat exploded in my ears.

Nothing.

Ahead of us Anna and Ben used their oars to tuck in close to the rubble bridge between the two buildings. Anna held the boat steady as Ben jumped ashore. The metal shrieked across the masonry. Ryan and I cringed. We all looked up at the few lighted windows. Ryan picked up the pace and settled us in behind them.

I looked down from the butt-hugging seat to the tumble of stonework. This was not going to be graceful.

I lifted myself up out of the seat and back onto the deck. I wriggled each foot free of Ryan, discovering them to be more than a little asleep. Ben scrambled forward. Clinging to his half-embrace, I managed to launch myself, trying not to shoot Ryan back out into the canal. I landed face-planted against Ben's chest, one foot on his, the other foot rolling a half-brick in circles. He stumbled back and I got my feet under me.

My old bodyguard pulled me in hard for the hug I had once forbidden. This time I hugged him back, wishing we had the time to slip off somewhere, wishing I could ask him what was wrong. Just the feel of him confirmed what I already knew: my friend was not okay.

I hugged him a little harder, then pulled away, not wanting Anna to misunderstand. We both hurried forward to help Ryan ashore. I offered Ryan my hand. He took it. I lost my breath at my own stupidity. Burning pain raced in tendrils up my arm. By the time he was steady on his feet, I was blind with tears.

Ryan took one look at my face and jerked his hand away.

"Shit, sorry," he whispered.

"No," I bit out. "Worse. Worse...than it used to be."

I gripped my wrist, tried to relax against it.

"We need to move the boats. We'll be leaving a different way," Anna said softly from somewhere nearby. I waved the boys away. I heard the crunch of rock and cleared my eyes, tried to shake my hand back to usefulness.

"I remember that part." I looked down at Anna's gentle eyes. "Here, let me see."

I held my hand out. She took it in her small, battered ones and began to rub it gently.

"It gets better if you decide to do the treatment. If you don't, it just keeps getting worse." She saw my eyes get wide. "There aren't too many regular people around here," she assured me.

The boys were coming back. She quickly dropped my hand. I gave it a quick test stretch. Whatever she'd done, it was functional again.

I pointed to the old prison behind them.

"We'll set up over there."

Ryan led the way out of sight.

Time to begin operation two-by-four.

Chapter 10

My friends were back.

Two little swarm cameras bobbed at the edge of my vision as I stood with Ben on the aquarium glass below Matteo's apartment window.

Give me a better look at the latch.

I stretched my hand up toward the second pane and one of the camouflaged orbs followed it. While Ryan analyzed the lock, I analyzed what I could see of the room inside. An open suitcase sat on the bed. He had it about half packed. We hadn't missed him yet. But I also had yet to glimpse him within either.

My kingdom for a hacksaw, Ryan grumbled.

What about this knife thingy you gave me?

It'll probably work, but you and Ben will have to time it just right or you'll just end up welding the thing back shut again.

Ben nodded at me and squatted down, cupping his hands to give me a boost. He could hear the conversation; he just couldn't reply without speaking.

I pulled Ryan's multi-tool from my pants pocket and launched myself up. The windowsill was narrow. Thank god I'd left my pack with Ryan and Anna. Clinging to the upper sill with one set of fingers, I activated the heat cutter. Within seconds it glowed white hot, the wood smoked, and I began to realize I stood a very good chance of setting the whole thing on fire. Quickly, I plunged the blade up between the two panes.

Yep, fire.

I yanked the blade against the latch and Ben shoved upward at the pane. The whipping wind egged the tiny fire on. My hair went flying in the same direction. I jerked the blade one more time, then wrested it free, and dropped back down to the aquarium glass. I switched the blade off, left to cool on the glass ledge where we stood. Ben and I both shoved at the window.

I felt it give. I looked to Ben.

One, two, three!

The last thread of metal gave way with a squeal and the window slid free.

Well, if he didn't already know we were here...

I grabbed for the sill.

Wait. Let me take a quick look around. That's why we brought them, remember?

Biting back an unreasonable surge of frustration, I sank down out of sight and Ben did the same. I raised my hand to the windowsill.

Let's see how rusty I really am, Ryan muttered. *Releasing cameras.*

The two little bumps in my view of the stone sill jerked and floated back from my hand and became two little bumps in my view of the palace wall. Then with an arching swish, they glided into the apartment. I lowered my hand.

I'm going to watch, I told Ben, letting him know he was effectively on guard duty.

I leaned my head against the wall for balance and closed my eyes.

Ryan's camera's scanned the largely empty bedroom and I went with them, sweeping into an open closet with only a jacket and a pair of t-shirts remaining, under a bed hiding a pair of mud-soaked sneakers, over a chair.... I hesitated, stared. Folded over the back of the chair, lay a rumpled tuxedo...and two scarlet gloves—mine. Ryan's cameras continued on, but I saw nothing except that red satin, that black grosgrain deep against it. That same fabric which had lain against my skin that cold night on the palace roof, that same fabric which had wrapped my senses in his scent and left my head floating.

I opened my eyes. Ben watched me, searching. I felt suddenly exhausted. He gripped my shoulder in question. I just nodded, tried to smile.

He's not there. I'm going in, gonna get ready for him to come back for that bag.

Alyse, wait for me to finish, Ryan ordered.

Ben's grip tightened on my shoulder. I smacked it away. He had no leverage up here on this ledge of glass. There was nothing he could do as I vaulted my way up and through the window.

Damn it, Alsye!

Part of me wanted to shut the window behind me.

For a moment, I stood there in the emptiness of his room, tasting the slight hollowness of a life that fit in such a small suitcase, a life where one or two family photos and an old book splayed on the nightstand were the sum of the emotional clutter of your life outside of work. That hollowness was a familiar refuge to me.

To see it in him brought me to a sad stillness.

I hadn't meant to. I'd meant to charge in and find a position behind the kitchen counter, somewhere out of his line of sight, somewhere I could hide until he'd closed the door fully behind him. I hadn't meant to drift over to that chair, drawn by the sad stillness. Hadn't meant to lift the gloves and set them aside. Hadn't meant to run my hand over that tuxedo jacket. The scent of him still clung to it.

I sighed.

"Alyse."

One whispered word and my heart moved from slow motion to the thunder of a raging storm. I had miscalculated.

Slowly, I turned to face him.

"Matteo."

Over jeans and a casual white button shirt, his tousled hair was damp, a white towel clutched between his hands. Those soft brown eyes regarded me in wonder.

"They said, you'd—"

I took a step forward and he cut himself off. His bare feet stumbled back a step and he held the bunched towel forward as a defense. With that single reaction, my heartbeat slowed to a steady, watchful rhythm. I took another step forward. He fell back another pace.

"Alyse," he begged and I saw his hands shaking now.

His beautiful face twisted and my heart twisted with it. Clawing, raking, scraping up the remains of my courage, I reached out and laid my hand on his. The tension left both our bodies and we drew together, connected only by that simple touch.

"Matteo," I whispered.

He closed his eyes. "I can't. I have to go to treatment. I have to go."

I felt the tremor in him at just the word.

"Do you want to?"

"I have to."

"Do you want to?"

I lifted his chin and he raised his gaze to mine. The agony there made my days of terror in looking forward to this reunion feel paltry and selfish. Anna was right. This all had fractured him soul-deep. It was almost as if I could see the dark cracks within him.

"Do you want to?"

"No, but I can't—"

"Then let's go. Where are your shoes?"

I released him and trotted back to his suitcase, zipped it closed.

"Ben!" I called.

Ben popped up from his post. He was thoroughly ready to kill me. That wasn't going to help get Matteo moving.

"We're ready here. Why don't you come on in and raid the kitchen?" I turned back to Matteo. "You don't mind, do you?"

Matteo just stared at Ben. I shifted to get in his line of sight.

"Matteo? Can we borrow some food?"

He nodded, still staring over my shoulder.

Ben, PR face NOW before we lose him!

Ben was a grinning idiot by the time he landed in Matteo's bedroom.

"Hey, buddy, got a bag for them groceries?" He clapped Matteo on the shoulder as he passed and the shell-shocked man followed him obediently into the kitchen. As Matteo watched Ben dump his cupboards, I ran back to the bathroom, grabbed a packed toiletries case and his socks. I found his shoes by the door, a pair of thick leather casual shoes with some good treads. Perfect for where we were going.

I shoved the shoes and socks at him as I came back through. In his bedroom, I pushed the toiletries bag inside the suitcase and tore through the closet until I found that winter coat. By the time I crammed that in too, the suitcase was no longer half full.

Hefting the suitcase, I swung it around and over to the doorway.

"That'll have to do. Come on!"

The two men grabbed the bags Ben had filled and filed out of the kitchen. Waiting at the window, I jerked my head toward it.

"You're taller. You go first," I told Ben. "I'll hand things down to you."

Ben cocked his head with its too cheerful smile.

"Absolutely!"

I was a dead woman.

Later.

Ben went over the side and Matteo dropped the first grocery bag to him, then the second. I jogged the suitcase higher in my grip. It grew abruptly heavier. I realized Matteo was pushing it back down.

"Alyse, I can't."

"You would rather stay here and let them—"

"If that's what it takes to never hurt you again. When I came to and found you on the floor, all the blood, and your arm," he closed his eyes and shook out his head, "when I realized...."

The heartbreak and the terror created an acid whirlpool in my stomach. It took more than I ever knew I had to hide my reaction. I kept my silence as I watched him.

"I can't go through this anymore," he whispered. "I'm done."

I let the suitcase lower between us.

This isn't about him.

And it wasn't about me either. I hung my head at Ryan's abrupt reminder. Gritting my teeth, I shifted my hold on the suitcase, yanked it out from under Matteo's hand and dropped it down to Ben.

Matteo gaped at me, then just shook his head.

"This doesn't change—"

"Matteo, somebody is fucking with the Syndrome. If we don't look out, it won't just be about us beating each other to a goddamn bloody pulp. It will be about more kids landing in those fucking castles. My team, we've got resources; we can figure this out, but we need you to come with us. We need your help."

"I can't."

"Then who will—," I cut myself off this time when I realized he was raising his pant leg. *Confined to his apartment.* I cursed my own stupidity.

Shit! I heard Ben echo Ryan's sentiment from down below. *The cutter, try the cutter.*

Without giving Matteo a chance to join the commentary, I swung myself out the window. Ben had taken the cutter from the ledge. He handed it up to me. Back inside I went.

I held the cutter up to Matteo.

"You're out of excuses." Then I took a step closer so I could look deeper into those achingly soft brown eyes. I released the demands from my voice, wrapped the cutter more tightly in my fingers. "Who are you going to be, Matteo Ranier? You have to decide. Who are you going to be?"

He stepped back from me again, sank to the bed. I could see the resignation in his body even as he tipped his head back to blink away the tears. Resignation, but not the will to fight. He lifted his pant leg again.

One step at a time.

I knelt before him and saw Ryan's cameras bobbing near his leg.

You should be able to drive the cutter straight down through the processor, but you'll need to do something to protect his leg. Ben, get up there and give her a hand.

I heard Ben's grunt as I rose. Something to protect his leg.

"Wait here a second."

I hurried to the kitchen and started rifling through drawers, tin foil, plastic, glass...a silicone potholder? I jogged back with it. Ben emerged through the window, looking exhausted this time. He knelt with me and helped me work it between the cuff and Matteo's leg. The poor man hissed as we took out probably half his leg hairs.

"Hold it," I instructed Ben.

Tell me I'm not about to smelt this thing to his leg!

I have no idea.

Shit.

I fired up the cutter.

You'll have to move fast. It will have a back up alarm. Security will show up real quick. And you'll have to get it all the way off. Tracking device.

Got it.

I angled my arm between Ben's and drove the blade home, then snapped it back toward me. My elbow caught Ben square in the solar plexus. He wheezed, but held steady. Digging his thumbs into the device, he cracked it the rest of the way open. I switched off the super-heated blade.

Ben got to his feet, tossed the cuff to the bed. I rose. I reached out my hand.

Matteo kept his hands clenched into the edge of the bed.

"We have to go. We can do this."

He raised his eyes only as far as my hand.

But he took it.

So warm, so strong enveloping mine. Again the tension fell away and I just savored that comfort as it ebbed and flowed up my arm like a steadily rising tide. He shifted his hand to more completely engulf mine. But he didn't look up.

"Come on," I said finally.

I drew him with me toward the window, found Ben staring at me. He raised his shocked eyebrows, flicked his gaze in the direction of my and Matteo's joined hands. I just shook my head.

Alyse, look out!

I spun around and found Dr. Roz and Jürgen Phan Mai standing in the door of Matteo's bedroom.

"Shit! Ben, get out! Get out!" I turned to Matteo. "Get him out!" I shoved him at my bodyguard. Apparently, Ben wasn't taking orders from me or Matteo. I slammed back against both of them.

Ben, if she touches you, you're done. Get your ass out of here!

"Alyse, honey, I told Jürgen I hadn't felt you leave. But then what does a little ol' lady know, anyway?"

Too much. I could already feel myself swaying and she was clear across the room.

"Stay back."

Dr. Roz folded her short, wrinkled fingers together over a cardigan of huge purple orchids. Her rounded poof of grey-blonde hair shown like a sun around twinkling eyes. Jürgen Phan Mai didn't look quite so benevolent.

"You cannot help him this way, Alyse. You do not understand the rules of this game." Wind whipped through the room, then one, two, three cracks of light flashed through the window. The sky opened up with a boom and the strike of rain rattled the glass behind me. The lights in the apartment flickered and died.

What are you guys doing? Get out of there! Now! Go! Ryan yelled.

Ben and Matteo stirred against my back and I shoved them again toward the window. But I couldn't turn my own gaze from Jürgen. The light and shadows of the storm were his.

He stepped forward, his sweeping eyebrow raised.

"Would you leave the circle again, Alyse? Would you run again? Do you crave your own destruction so much? And this time you would take these two with you. Have you no love for them at all?" He raised an elegant hand to gesture toward Matteo and Ben. Only then did I realize how close he had come.

I scrambled back. Frantic, I beat against Ben with elbows and heels. It was no longer a matter of keeping him safe. He was between me and the window.

Maybe they had been caught up in the same rapture, because I felt them jerk to life behind me. We were a tangle of sharp-boned limbs and battered ribs as the two of them clambered over the sill, me keeping my eyes on the doctor and the mayor, terrified that if I glanced back, even for a second, they'd have me.

My seeking hands hit the stone. I scooted back onto it. But then I had to shift to swing my legs around. Dangling half way out of the window, she caught me.

Light flooded my body, my consciousness. A looseness and a floating release. Yet somehow her single, small hand kept me from falling.

"Alyse, my child, my dear little one, this is not the way to save him. This is not the way to save yourself."

My head rolled and the sudden movement helped me grasp after my faculties. I raised my hand to her makeup-caked face, so comforting, so...

"It's not about us." The fog of forest light swam in my vision, green with swaying leaves. I shook my head and saw a glimpse of Jürgen reaching for me. Again, I reached for the point, the point of it all.

"It's not about us. It's about the children."

I reared back and shoved against the frame. Jürgen's fingers interrupted the wind as they brushed past me. Dr. Roz's hold broke. Yellow lightning cracked a black sky as I fell back over the ledge.

And down.

Chapter II

I landed on them.

But this was not their first stunt.

They absorbed some of the energy of my long, slow fall; redirected the rest of it. If the rain made their holds on my arms, on my legs slippery, my slippery grasp on the solidity of reality made the culmination of my landing more bloody than necessary.

I lay there, staring up at the wild sky. The rain struck my face and some of the wet was wrongly warm. A surreal dance of lightning shot through those darkly whirling clouds. *Lucifer, do you guide your witches home?* In time with the thought, Jürgen drew my gaze to him, framed by that faraway window, his regard regal and distant, terrifying.

Why? I wanted to beg him. *Why did you do this to me? Tell me, please.* But I was no longer sure of his place in any of it, no longer sure of my place in any of it.

It was Ben who pulled me free of the rock I had become a part of. Matteo drew back from me, his lips turning grey. He grabbed

Anna's arm. Gently, she freed herself and wrapped her own arm around his waist. Without words, my boys, my steadfast brothers led me to the aluminum boat. Anna guided Matteo to her kayak.

Once more we were water-borne.

∽

The canals became frigid, wind-whipped tunnels as we descended deeper and deeper into the ruins. The entire façade of a palace created a ceiling overhead, dripping with fine, white roots. We huddled together warily in our narrow craft as we passed beneath, those albino hairs brushing stiffly at our own. Paddles switched to awkward poles, less propelling us forward, more guiding us alongside unsteady walls glimpsed in flashes of lightning.

Our boat jarred against the kayak. I raised my rain-soaked gaze to see the skeleton of a costume boutique tumbled into our path. Matteo pulled free of the kayak, his long, dark hair and thin, white shirt heavy with rain. I watched the music of his movement as he drew first Anna, then the kayak from the water.

He did not look back to me.

I did not expect him to.

Ryan guided us to that same spot. Ben jerked out from behind me. I fell back against his bench. Blinking with surprise, I pushed myself carefully upright to find Ryan looking back at me with a raised eyebrow. I ignored him and took my own leave of the boat. Ryan tossed my pack after me. Together with Ben he lifted our craft and followed the path Matteo and Anna had taken.

I followed behind them, more on all fours than two. This was a newly fallen building and still clung to the form it had held in life. I climbed past the first arcade of windows. Papers fluttered to the water that filled the side wall. I watched faded images of glittering Carnival revelers jerk and tremble as they took the blows of rain and slowly sank down, down into the murk. A scrap of gold curtain fluttered in the next set of windows. The metallic threads of its remains snapped in the wind that tossed my own hair and raised the ripple of chill under my skin.

I paused to let the shudder dissipate.

The stone beneath my knees shifted.

I grasped after the solidity of the marble windowsill. Too late. Like rigid paper, the thin stone façade folded at the seam. With me inside it. My own weight ripped the sill from my fingers.

"Shit!"

I flailed, managed to catch hold of a cloth cord, but it was attached to nothing. The wall, the window, we fell together toward the toxic water, that cord grasped tightly in my hand. I closed my eyes, stretched out my arms, trying to protect myself from whatever lay beneath that murk.

I hit the water.

The sting was instant, the side of my head, my hands, my ribs.

Then I was sucked downward. No, not sucked. Those were hands. They pulled at my clothes, at my hair, pulled me deeper under.

My eyes flew open. Darkness.

I fought back, kicking, punching. Something huge and heavy hit my hip. The wall. I heard the muted roar. The whole building!

I let myself go limp. Those hands, they were everywhere, pulling, dragging, hurtling me forward. Chunks of stone pelted my sensitized skin as those hands jerked me back and forth through the maze of the collapsing caverns.

And then we stopped. For an instant I floated blind, as if standing in a cloud of gritty vapor. The guiding hands relaxed. Slowly, slowly those invisible palms began gliding over me. One slid down the length of my arm, explored the separation of my fingers. Another pair gently ran down my left leg, removing the bent tension of my knee and ankle, finding the nakedness of my foot, invading every crevice with penetrating strokes. Yet another freed my hair and played in the billowing silk. My useless eyes began to drift close. The hand at the hem of my shirt pressed up my torso until it lifted the tender weight of my right breast.

Something in me snapped awake.

Something in me realized I was drowning.

My lungs seized and again I was struggling against caresses which had become ruthless holds. I struck out with the limbs I could move. What I hit was slender, solid, unmoving. I fought against my own body, desperate for that one breath that would end me.

And then my vision snapped on.

He floated before me, his long black hair whirling around those hard, alien eyes. Those large white hands reached for my face, grasped me tenderly. Then he took me by the mouth.

And breathed into me.

The restraining hands clutching the rest of my body wriggled, vanished.

Just his remained, holding me just long enough, just until I was filled.

Then he released me.

And I floated away.

Chapter 12

I broke the surface like walking into the middle of a holographic movie—out of darkness and silence and stillness: chaos. Shouts hit my ears, huge raindrops slapped my frozen skin, color and shape struck my eyes, frantic reality slammed through my veins. Now the straps of my sodden pack threatened to pull me under, now the strain of my lungs had me clutching my chest. I twisted desperately, trying to find something, someone to hold onto before I slipped under again.

"Alyse! Ben, there she is!"

I turned toward the sound of Anna's voice, just barely got my hand up as the grocery boat slid right next to my head. Ben's dark hand instantly wrapped around my wrist, he pulled, but it was like trying to pull the canal out from under him.

"My pack." Could he even hear that harsh, painful whisper over the thunder and rain?

A yellow wall slid up along the other side of my head.

Someone got hold of the handle of my backpack.

"Just a second, I'm going to end up pulling out half her hair. No, stay on the other side of the boat, I've got it." Ryan. It was Ryan.

"Matteo?" I croaked. Did he make it?

No one answered.

I clung to Ben's winter-weave wrapped wrist until I felt the weight of my pack rise. One limb at time, I pulled myself free of it. Then I reached for the edge of the silver boat; a second set of hands grabbed me and the boat dipped dangerously. The rim of the craft caught me just under the rib and those hands rolled me the rest of the way in.

Those soft, sad brown eyes, those lips parted in exertion. My Venetian. He was alive. He searched my face, reached up and touched the side of my head. His fingers came back red.

Anna appeared at his shoulder and he showed her the stain.

"Hagebak. Do you know where he is now?" Matteo asked.

Anna sat back and I could hear her blow out a breath.

"God, I think he's holed up in the church across the campo. We're all going to need him now."

I pushed at the boat, trying to sit up. I froze halfway up. My head.

"I've got an onboard. I don't need...I don't need a doctor." I reached behind me, ended up grabbing Ben's leg, but I got myself upright.

"Adriatic fever. You get that and you're done. Alyse, careful." Matteo caught my arm and I frowned at him. Then I realized I wasn't actually sitting upright—and that I was shaking the entire boat.

"Anna, get in that kayak with Army Boy," Ben ordered. "You need to be gettin' us outta here."

Matteo handed Anna to Ryan. I wasn't the only one shivering. We all were. Anna took over the kayak's oar. Ryan ...Ryan clutched his shoulder. Injured. *Oh, shit.*

Matteo had the oars for our boat. He waited until Anna scraped past and then dipped them in. The canal was too narrow to use the oars properly, but he seemed accustomed to it. The two carriers glided us down just a short length of urban canyon and then turned into a wider area—maybe once a dock or courtyard, judging by the menacing remains of buildings jutting up through the water.

But Anna and Matteo seemed to know their way through the dangers hidden by the dark, pelted water.

And then, in another flash of lightning, the way before us opened up completely. Our boats shot forward into a huge, blinding lake surrounded by the maroons, bronzes, and coppers of largely intact buildings. Anna turned us and before the light flickered out, I saw a church with its entire center entry cut out like someone had sliced the building down the middle with a titan-sized sword.

As we drew closer, the church's mutilated face grew clearer. Great gouges in the stone gaped down at us like wounds and I found myself pushing with my hands and feet against the forward motion of the boat. Neither of our two Venetians noticed as they slid us into that dark, deep maw.

The pounding of the rain against my body stopped.

I relaxed against the darkness. One building collapse a night. That had to be statistically fair. I caught my shoulders rising and lowered them again.

The boat crashed against something. Matteo cursed. Ben and I scrambled to catch ourselves and each other—me clutching his leg, him grasping my arm.

"Stop. Stay here," Anna whispered. "I'll see if I can find him."

I heard her climb out of the kayak, saw the vague silhouette of her ascending some kind of...big grey shape. I concentrated on the sound of her progress until it blended too well with the thud and thunder of the storm. It felt strange to be relying on the cottage garden flower of the group. But I already knew Grocery Girl was tougher than she looked.

Mo, where are we?

Chiesa di Santa Maria Formosa. Then my AI proceeded to translate.

I accidentally laughed.

Ben's shivering hand released my arm.

"What?" he demanded.

I waited until Mo finished the story.

"Ben, this is your kind of church," I whispered. "Church of the Buxom Saint Mary."

"Nice."

I even heard Ryan and Matteo chuckle quietly.

"Apparently when Venice was still mostly swamp, this really busty apparition of the Virgin Mary came to St. Magnus and told him to build a church to her where a white cloud settled on the ground. Mo says this St. Magnus guy had a penchant for daydreaming. Seven other churches in Venice were also founded because of his visions."

"This place is seriously called the Church of the Virgin Mary of the Big Tits?"

"Dude, you are so going to get struck by lightning," Ryan hissed. But he didn't stop laughing.

The beam of a flashlight speared me right in the cornea, then proceeded to bob across the dark. I pressed a frozen hand to my eyes and sparks shot across my abused vision.

"He's here. Come on," I heard Anna's disembodied voice call out. I guessed we were no longer whispering.

When I released my eyes, the light illuminated a crumpled square pillar, flecked with red. Ryan was closest to it. One-handed he used the paddle to pull back over to it. With a quick jerk, he switched his grasp on the paddle for a grip on the pillar—same hand. Just how injured was he?

He managed to yank himself from the boat to the pillar and dragged the kayak behind him for a few butt scoots. Then he had to pause, head hanging.

Not good.

I pulled my legs from the bench in front of me. I couldn't feel my feet hit the floor of the boat. Shaking out my head, I waited for the blood to level out.

"Stay there," I ordered.

"Oh, I'll fish de boy oot."

A colossal pair of hiking boots appeared beside Ryan. A thick, knit-sweatered arm lowered and a gloved hand pulled the kayak from my camera operator's grip. The boat left the circle of light. I heard it settle; then the man lowered himself next to Ryan.

"Here ya go, *dens*. De good stuff's just a leetle distance over dees columns here."

I blinked. Something about the way that narrow shaft of light caught his thick white hair, left part of his craggy face in shadow. He reached an arm around Ryan and lifted him easily to his feet. A few steps and they were gone from the island of light. I stared at the spot where they had been.

"He'll be alright."

I raised my eyes and Matteo held my gaze until the tension fell from my eyes. I nodded ever so slightly. I would trust them. I had to. I had no way to help Ryan and there was no way I would even consider bringing him back to Dr. Franco at the palace.

Matteo turned back and used one of the paddles to drag us closer to the fallen pillar. The light bobbed and shivered. Anna was coming to help.

Her small white hands caught the bow of the boat as it tossed with our collective tremors and the distant rhythm of the storm-ravaged sea. Matteo tucked away the oars. The usual music of his movement turned sluggish and stiff as he forced one leg over the side and shifted his weight to it, then dragged the other leg out, balancing against Anna. He took her place as anchor and she scooted back to give the rest of us room and light.

My turn.

I pushed up off the bench, driving shards of ice up the palms and wrists of hands I could not feel. I only gained a few centimeters. Ben pushed me from behind and I clenched my teeth, drove every muscle into straightening my legs until the tendons in the backs of my knees tried to tear. Hooking my hands over the edge of the boat, I stumped my legs forward into Matteo's section. I took a good, hard look at the narrow column where he was perched. I could hear the way their breath rattled, Ben, Matteo, and Anna. I knew I needed to hurry.

"Ben, move the suitcase to the other side again," Matteo chattered.

I shifted my weight to my hands as the boat tilted.

"Come on, baby. You got this. Just one leg and then the other. I gotta stay over here or we'll both go swimmin' again."

I took a deep breath and heaved. My shin clocked the edge of the boat, my thumb wrenched free of the side.

"Dere, *liten jente*. No more swimmin' for you."

Warmth caught me under the arms, lifted me up. I heard my legs scrape free of the boat. I looked up, the towering old man smiled gently down at me. His left eye caught me, though, ice-blue and shining like the glaciers hinted of in his voice. I drew that light into me, ice-bright, chill, and clean like a breeze that remembered Nature at her purest. A subtle scent of ocean and pine. I breathed it in.

The man's shining eye widened, then narrowed in curiosity as he lowered me to the pillar. My body jarred and I realized my feet must have hit ground.

"Woot it harm your womanly pride, if I carried you to my office?"

"Hagebak, if it's alright, let's worry about her pride later. She drank half the canal," Matteo said between shrieks of metal.

The Norwegian swung my lower half into his other arm and began to lead the way up rubble. I heard other footsteps behind us. My womanly pride kept my head upright as we jarred from one chunk of church to the next, until my vision started sparking, then clouding with its own darkness.

"Rest, *liten jente*. We're almost dere."

I closed my eyes and leaned my head gingerly against his shoulder, but even there the darkness swirled around me. I could feel it brushing my cheek, rushing around my torso, my legs. There was something so familiar about it. I reached for it, so close, what was it? But then a different darkness blanketed my mind, my body.

And it was gone.

Chapter 13

My eyes opened.

Through sparks and blots of darkness I saw that the Norwegian was settling me on the floor. Warm, the floor was warm.

"I will bring you girls de wash and de towels."

His shadow retreated along with the rich, icy scent of him. I turned my head and saw Anna shuddering next to me. Blue framed pale lips and drew the natural rose-garden color from her cheeks. She looked down at me.

"My god, Alyse! How much blood have you lost?"

Did I look that bad? I didn't feel that bad. I didn't feel anything.

"I don't...I don't know. I need my pack."

"I'll get it. It's on the stairs."

She rose and walked out of our small stone room. I pushed myself carefully upright. Our room was empty, but well-maintained with a smooth, solid wood floor and a sturdy window. A pipe with a vent ran up the side. The left side of my body told me the pipe was where the heat originated.

Anna returned and dropped herself and my sodden pack to the floor. I reached for it, but the Norwegian's voice stopped me.

"You need to disinfect it first. You need someting from de bag?"

"Medicine for my medical implant."

"Ah, dis is waterproof?"

I nodded.

He lowered a pot of water, a pair of towels and washcloths, and a cup of herbs and salts to the floor. "Before you take de medicine, you will drink de tea. Too many toxins in your body right now."

I dropped my hand down into my lap.

"Where are Ben and Ryan and Matteo?"

The old man raised his head with a smile. "De gentlemen wash in de otter room. When you finish, I will take you down. I will leave de tea outside your door."

"Thank you, Dr. Hagebak," Anna said.

Hagebak.

He rose with one eyebrow high. "You bring me interesting patients, Miss Parks."

With one last inquisitive look in my direction, he left us to clean up.

Anna dumped the cup of herbs into the steaming pot, then began undressing. I followed her lead. Wordlessly, we designated a spot by the door for sea-soaked clothes. Trying to leave Anna her privacy, I struggled with the single trainer on my left foot, both the sock and shoe from my right foot residing at the bottom of a collapsed costume shop back in the canal.

No shoes. Not good. How the hell was I going to replace them?

"We'll get some new ones. But you need to get cleaned up. Adriatic fever sets in fast and you are covered with gashes."

I blinked my way back from thoughts of shoeless flights across jagged rubble, blood seeping up through my toes. I glanced back at her. Already stripped to the waist, small breasts puckered with the cold, she struggled with her own shoes. I watched her pause, flexing her fingers, trying to coax enough movement into stiff joints to manipulate the laces.

"Here."

I grabbed her shoe by the heel and yanked. It took a couple jerks and her eyes were tearing by the end, but we got both of them off.

"Thanks."

I pointed to a red blush starting at her neck and beginning to creep its way up to her face and across her chest and shoulders.

"Adriatic fever?'

She raised a hand to her throat, then jerked her hand away.

"Yes, damnit!"

Reacting to her sudden frantic struggle to free herself from the rest of her clothes, I grappled with mine as well. The button on my cargoes was nearly impossible, the zipper, like holding the sharp end of a knife. Anna reached the pot of steeping herbs first and began slathering herself using one of the washcloths. I grabbed a washcloth as well and though the heat stung my skin and the salts burned the open wounds that seemed to be everywhere, I didn't feel the pain Anna seemed to. Her rash flashed a brilliant red now, migrating steadily down her small torso.

"Is this normal?"

"No, I must," she paused to bite back a groan, "I must have too many cuts."

I heard a small clatter at the door.

"Will the tea help?"

"Yes."

I scrambled for the door, fell to my knees as my vision began flashing even harder. I needed Margie. He said I had to drink the tea first. I crawled my way to the door, released the handle and hoped whoever was on the other side didn't mind getting flashed.

The stairs were empty. I grabbed one cup and scooted my way back to Anna. Where the shaking in my hands had receded, hers shook so wildly now she couldn't take the cup from me. I held the cup to her lips and gave it a slight tip. She choked.

"Nope, that's not what we're doing, Grocery Girl. Down the hatch. Come on."

I gave it another try. This time she got some down. A little break. Then some more. A choking spell. Her skin had turned scarlet down to her wrists and hips now. A rattle of panic began to warm me from the inside.

"Come on, kid. The rest."

She just managed to swallow it before the choking cough doubled her over completely. I set the cup aside.

"Did you miss washing off anything?"

"My, my back!"

I grabbed her washrag and turned her as she lost herself to another round. Good god, her back was a mottled purple. She jumped as I ran the water down that tortured skin. I tried to delicately wipe it down between her jerks and cries.

The last round of coughing subsided and she collapsed to her side on the floor, shaking. I snagged one of the towels and patted at her face and hair. If I could get her dry, I could wrap her in the fur blanket in my pack. That had to help.

She slapped at me.

"Finish yourself."

I glanced back at the pot. Right. I tucked the towel around as much of her as it would cover and found my own washcloth tucked behind the pot. I doused myself in the weed-scented water, soaking it as deep into my long hair as I could, scrubbing at every piece of skin I could reach. The water was turning a deep pink. I frowned, looking down at my washcloth. Blood red.

Now.

I needed Margie now.

I crawled back over to my cup of tea. In one, long pull, I finished the whole thing. My stomach instantly cramped around the heat and the strange, bitter herbs. Fighting to keep it down, I dragged my naked ass back over to the pot and my pack that sat nearby. Disinfect it. I didn't know how disinfected it would get with bloody water, but tough shit.

I used Anna's rag and resoaked the black cloth cover of the bag, taking extra care around the zipper seal. My stomach was heaving now. Careful to avoid any drips, I unsealed the bag and peeled back the cover. The blanket filled most of the bag. I worked it free and tossed it to a dry corner.

"Anna, come on. I've got a blanket for you."

She tried to raise her head.

"Nope, that's not good enough. Let's go."

I shoved at her foot and she kicked back. But she got to her hands and knees and before long I had her settled and wrapped tightly in the fur. Her shuddering released with a sigh.

"Thank you, Alyse."

Thank you for nearly getting her killed? Yeah, great. But the ruddiness was fading from her cheeks and her breathing slowly began to taken on a more natural rhythm. I released a sigh of my own and some of that painful panic released from my shoulders. Even my stomach calmed a bit. But that wouldn't last.

I pulled myself back over to the pack and fished the zipper pouch from the bottom. Matteo's gift to me: my specialty vitamins and minerals for feeding Margie's nanobots. Just a few of them. I hadn't wanted to rattle when we conducted our surveillance. The bottles were back at the monastery with the rest of our things.

Because I wasn't taking them regularly, because these weren't direct-to-the-bloodstream poppers, this was going to hurt. A lot.

A rivulet of herb-water ran into my eye. I hissed and brushed it away. I lowered my hand. Not herb-water. Blood.

Mo?

Yes.

I need you to turn Margie on just as soon as these minerals hit my system whether I'm conscious or not.

Acknowledged.

I opened the zipper pouch and pulled out two capsules of vitamins and two capsules of minerals. At least this time my stomach wasn't completely empty. Mostly.

I had to dry-swallow them. The bottle of water Ryan had given me was floating down the canal somewhere. I tried not to brace myself, instead wrapping up in my own towel and taking a moment of peace next to the heater vent. Eyes closed, I leaned my head back and listened to the rain and thunder like it was music. If I quieted my breathing, I could even hear the voices of the men below. No cries of pain, just the murmur of conversation. Ryan's shoulder. Maybe it wasn't as bad as it seemed. What had happened in those missing moments? Had they been caught like...

I hissed as Margie tingled to life beneath my left rib. Again I tried not to brace myself as her little repairmen pushed out and up along my spine, ravenous little scavengers that would turn rabid once they reached their worksites. It wasn't unlike having tiny little drills excavating along all your bones and arteries. I let myself slide to the floor, tried to detach myself from my body, hummed to cover up the pain. I'd only experienced this on a minor scale in my professional life. I'd never had to leave Margie to starve before.

For a split second I forgot to stay detached. The pain got its hooks into me. The cry clawed its way up my throat. I smothered it with my hands, arched my entire body against it. Gasping, fighting for breath, I tried to pull my mind away. Leave, leave. Somewhere cold and bright.

Fire!

Fire, everywhere!

I screamed.

๑

"Alyse!"

Ben's big hands pinned my shoulders down as I thrashed.

"Alyse, what's going on?"

"M-Margie. Oh, god! Don't touch me!"

"Shit!" He snatched his hands away. "What? You used her this morning and nothing happened."

"Diagnostic."

"And this is a repair." Ryan's voice.

"Can she not turn dese ting off?"

"It should stabilize after a few minutes, I think," Ben answered.

"Did she take the pills I sent?"

Matteo. For a brief second the pain lulled.

"Yes," I whispered from my quiet darkness. I curled up there, held it tightly around me.

But deep inside the fire began to build again.

"....quick release. Should kick in..."

I gritted my teeth, but the scream ripped free anyway. The splotches of darkness that had covered my vision now covered my consciousness as well, blotting out patches of thought and sound. Just not blotting out the pain.

Someone straightened my towel. I just whimpered.

"...days has she been off the medication?"

"I don't know, maybe..."

They talked and they talked, but they didn't make it stop. So much pain. Everywhere. How could I be conscious? Too much pain!

A blanket? A fucking blanket? I kicked at it, smacked at it. So hot, so cold my teeth chattered.

"*Liten jente,* look at me. You are strong. Look at me, *liten jente.*"

I escaped the blanket. I caught after my frantic breathing. I forced my eyes open. I looked into the ice-glow of that gleaming left eye. I drew in that chill forest air.

"Make it stop," I begged.

"I am taking you down to my office, now. Be strong for me, now."

Stillness. Stillness.

The blanket tucked around me again. He lifted me. Ben helped him.

Stillness.

The stairs. Don't move. My breathing. Slow down. I bit my lips between my teeth.

"You are strong. Just a few more steps. No, no relax. You will fall."

"I can't."

"Yes, you can. Look at me. Open your eyes and look at me. Haf you effer been to *Norge?* You woot lof it dere. Blue sky so clear you tink you will float away in it. De old stories hiding in de trees. Ah, I see you like stories. We haf stories of a woman who hides in de trees. Huldra, she is named. She has de blonde hair, beautiful face like you. Ah, but she has de cow's tail she hides under her...her dress. Sometimes she is fery helpful, but if you are unkind to her, she is dangerous. Her faforite hobby is seducing de handsome young men away from deir camps and into her trees where dey must work fery hard to make her happy."

The doctor wiggled his eyebrows at me with a grin.

I chuckled at his joke.

We crossed the threshold to another small room. He lowered me carefully into a bed. His bed—the pine and ocean scented breezes.

"De pain is less now?"

I nodded.

"You sleep. You washed goot?"

Again, I nodded, my hand fluttering involuntarily beneath the blanket. He patted it down.

"I will find clotes and food for you when you wake up. *Drøm søtt.*"

A real bed. I let the softness and the sea breezes pull me down. *Drøm søtt.*

Chapter 14

"Holt dis."

I wasn't done sleeping. I rolled my head to the side and peeked through my eyelashes. Not me. Matteo was "holting dis," a shim of wood prying the metal vambrace away from his arm. In the dim glow of an averted flashlight, he sat opposite the doctor with a fishing tackle box full of packets and vials between them. The doctor uncapped a large vial and dipped a long medical swab into the oil.

A huge smell filled the room. Not exactly awful, more like a non-flowering woodland meadow in concentrate—with a strong hit of mint beneath it. Hagebak slathered the oil over Matteo's forearm beneath the brace, then threaded an adhesive bandage through, peeled the backing away, and sealed the oil inside. Matteo slowly, carefully pulled the shim free as the doctor locked his medicines and tools away.

Through a veil of lashes I watched Matteo's jeweled vambrace flash as he flexed his fist, then shook out his hand.

"God, forgot how much it stings!"

Hagebak reached out and tapped one of the stones. "You lost one."

I saw Matteo twist as if to turn and I quickly closed my eyes.

"She was going to die, Hagebak."

"Maybe it was her time."

"No, not just for trusting me. She didn't deserve to die. Not for that."

There was a long silence. Then a sigh.

"*Liten* Matti, dose children are not dead. Dey will lif again. You loose your belief too easily."

"Tell that to their parents."

"I tell dat to you. Dis medicine only makes de pull weak. De rest is belief. Tree years wit no jewels lost, no piece of your soul lost. Tree years and den you begin to loose your belief again. And now she pays the price wit you. Is dis better dan what you took away from her?"

"I didn't know!"

Hagebak only grunted.

"Did Cirena do this to her? She swears she didn't, but I don't trust her. I don't...."

A big, gentle hand smoothed my hair back from my face. Hagebak's voice was very near when he answered.

"I do not tink dey can do dis. Maybe not. She is different from you and de otter patients. She smells of shatet woots and mountain sunlight. She smells of leetle creeks and blooming life. But she carries det wit her, too. She is heafy wit it."

That huge warmth moved away. I heard the tackle box scrape the floor. Boots thudded toward the door.

"Death. She seemed so sad that night. While I was locked in my apartment, I looked up why. Her father's funeral was last week."

Just last week?

"He was mauled by a shark out on—"

"A shark?" The boots twisted abruptly.

"What?"

"Notting maybe." Hagebak sighed heavily. "Maybe notting, maybe too much. Be careful wit dis girl, Matti. Her soul is in your hands and you haf only a few pieces of your soul left to bargain wit. Her soul, Matti."

The silence grew heavy. The door closed.

The blankets shifted around me. Matteo's hand, strong and long-fingered, slipped beneath my own and just cradled it. His hand that held my soul. I listened to the shuddering breaths; I listened to those breaths deepen into sobs.

I shifted in my "sleep" and took his hand in mine.

"Alyse?" he whispered.

I didn't respond. I wasn't ready. I knew finally who had messed with his meds, but now I had no idea what it meant.

᪥

Beautiful, warm, rich sunlight. I stretched out in a bath of it, reached out into every muscle in my body and opened myself up to it, drank it in. I felt...good, really good, so alive and at peace at the same time. I glanced over and saw that the room was empty, save for a cup of tea steaming on the windowsill.

I sat up and let the blankets fall away, wrinkled my nose. A stench like an old bale of hay interrupted my perfect moment. I swung my feet over the edge of the bed and then jerked them back again. A pot of water, a wash cloth, and a change of clothes. With shoes.

I was in love.

With somebody.

I sank down next to the water and breathed in the floral steam. This time I took it slow, savoring the release of my skin from the stiff crackle of sweat and disinfectant water. The doctor had added a subtle oil to the bath that left behind a smooth suppleness and the remembrance of wildflowers. Hand over hand, I worked it into my long hair, apologizing to the towel as I released a catch of dirt, small stones, and endless tangles.

When my hair finally swung freely and the water dripping to the towel ran clear, I rose and stretched again. I felt ready to fly, to float away, my muscles were so loose and comfortable. I reached for the clothes and stumbled. I caught myself on the edge of the bed.

Alarmed, I touched the side of my forehead. But no, Margie's work was done. The skin on my temple was smooth and soft from the oil.

Blood loss.

That explained this floating serenity. Margie could repair structure, but she couldn't replace blood supply. Only a good meal and time could help with that.

Margie.

Was it going to be like that every time from now on? I had experienced an entire palate of pain in my profession. I had never once screamed for someone to make it stop. A blush rose in my cheeks at the memory. But without Lone Pine Pictures' resources I couldn't keep her running at all times. Just feeding her on a per-use basis would be tricky. Mo used fewer resources, but even she had to be fed once a week. I winced as I thought of the bottle back at our base camp.

First things first.

Mo, please create a procedure for using Margie with only these pills on a per-use basis.

Acknowledged.

I sighed and began slicking the water from my skin since I had wasted the towel as a dirt catcher. Coaxing the simple black bra and panties on over my damp skin, I eyed the rest of the outfit. The cloth flowed over my fingers as I lifted the brown tunic. It looked long enough, but the cut hinted at an off-the-shoulder number with three-quarter length sleeves. The black leggings were cut of the same luxurious fabric.

The minute I walked out of this room, I was going to miss my winter-weave and cargoes.

I pulled on the rest of the outfit, the socks and boots being of equally exquisite quality. Somebody here had money.

Only one thing left me mildly unsettled: it all fit.

Right down to the bra.

With my light head overfilled with thought, I wandered to the window and, leaning my temple against the sill, cradled the cup of tea between my hands. I had Mo pull up a picture of the Catacomb of the Sleepers.

The image released by the U.N. only showed half of the circular room that had been revealed after the bombing in Turin. The stone walls were honeycombed with Sleepers veiled in shadow. The grouping in the center, the king, the queen, and their princess, lay in regal repose in a halo of light. With a flick of my fingers, I rotated the picture, zoomed in to those eerily perfect faces—so similar and yet so different from the faces of those children in the Castles.

Golden sunlight, moonless dark, and their daughter, the twilight that lay between.

What happened to you? Are you even human anymore; were you ever human? If Dr. Hagebak is right and the children really will awaken, will they be human when they do? I wanted to believe him, that man whose eye shown with glacier light, who carried the secrets of the forest in his scent.

But if he was the one messing with Matteo's meds...

...then wasn't he the one to blame for what had happened to me?

Some kind of freakish drug interaction?

That didn't seem quite right. I sipped at my tea as I stared at those three faces. Those carriers that go feral with their soulless eyes; is that what you were? Again, not quite right. Jürgen with his regal, terrible majesty, that seemed closer.

But then I remembered that moment in the hall, his weight crushing me to the floor, his face pressed against mine.

I must thank you, Alyse, for a beautiful hunt.

The feral was not completely gone, even from him.

What were you?

I understood that the carriers held bits of the princess's DNA within them, that it might somehow affect them, but what was my relationship to these ancient royals? My DNA patch: similar, but not exactly the same. What did that mean?

A king, a queen, their adult daughter, their entire court. No sign of disease, no injuries...and not a single child among them. Where were the children? I thought of my own parents, how heartbroken my mother looked when I left promising to return in three days time. And now I would never be returning to her. How could I ever find the strength to tell her she'd just lost her husband and daughter both?

I'd told Mo to place the call before I entirely realized what I was doing.

"Alyse?"

Mom had obviously been asleep. Even her avatar looked bleary. I pulled up a mountain scene, a fallen tree with a creek running alongside. I led the way and settled on the rough bark. She sank down beside me.

"Mom, are you enjoying your visit?"

"Alyse, what's the matter."

"I won't be able to come home for a while." If there was hope for the children, couldn't I borrow a bit for myself?

"What's going on?"

"I've gotten myself into some trouble. I'm trying to get it fixed, but it might be a while."

Mom turned her china doll face to the creek and studied the water.

"A while."

"A long while. I can't leave the country."

Her face bobbled a bit. I scooted closer. Here in this alternate universe I could put an arm around her with no consequences. I pulled her tight.

"I wanted to be there for you."

"I see him everywhere, Alyse."

"I know, I do, too. I'm so sorry, Mom. I didn't mean for this to happen."

"Alyse." My mom straightened. "You've been running for years, since Grandpa Don died. I expected this. I just hoped...hoped...hoped to have the luxury of someone to lean on for once. Just this once."

"Mom." Amazing that I could be a head taller than her and still feel so small.

I dropped my arm. I propped my elbows on my knees and studied the ripples in the clear water as it shaped its way along the smooth, colorful stones in the bright light. What could I say to that much pain? I was such an idiot. She already knew she'd lost both her daughter and her husband. She just thought she'd lost the daughter years ago.

I thought about that night on the pier of the Doge's Palace with the pack of ferals backing me to the water. She had no idea how hard I'd tried to get back to her. No idea how hard I'd fought.

And failed.

I rose and looked down at my pretty, precise little mother. She looked so tired, staring out at the virtual air before her. I squatted down to interrupt that empty gaze.

"I'm sorry I can't be there. I'll call as often as I can, but for now consider the condo yours. I'll have Mo turn my accounts over to you."

"I have my own money."

"I know."

"I don't need—"

"I know, but for now this is all I can do. Please take it."

"I'd rather have my daughter."

I reached up and wiped away her avatar's tears. "You do have your daughter. But I need my mother, too."

Simone Arlington Bryant closed her eyes and hung her head. "I'm sorry. I'm not sleeping...I'm...."

"I know. You know you don't need to worry about that with me. I've never expected you to be perfect." Unlike the rest of her world.

The gratitude I glimpsed as she reassembled herself hurt my heart so bad. The mayor's daughter, the world-class reporter's wife. What would she find, what would I find with all of that stripped away? A flash of Simone Arlington Bryant with a swing of neon blue hair and ripped jeans flickered through my head. I kept my laugh to myself.

With a jerk of my head as invitation, we both rose and started picking our way through the pebbles on the creek's narrow bank.

"Can you at least return Emory's calls? He said you aren't answering and he's worried. We're both worried. Tamsin is back, but she won't tell us anything. I've never known that girl to be so tight-lipped."

"She can't talk about it and neither can I. We're doing what we can to take care of things, but the more you and Emory stay out of it, the easier it will be for us. I'm serious about this. If Emory gets Lone Pine involved, I may never get out of here."

Her eyes searched my face as if she could find the answers to her forbidden questions in my expression. I kicked a rounded red stone out into the water, changed the subject.

"Is Emory keeping you company?"

Still searching, she nodded. "And your Aunt Rebecca was just here." A guilty smile. "She believes in retail therapy."

So my apartment was now full of candles, crystals, and hand-dyed draperies. I just shook my head and stepped over a sodden branch.

"Someday you will tell me exactly what I really did to dear Cousin Gabriela to ensure Aunt Becca only ever visits in my absence."

Mom laughed. "She does seem to have an unerring sense for when you will be gone, doesn't she? Somehow I think Gabriela has probably outgrown the nightmares by now."

I chuckled. A six-year-old with access to Grandpa Don's Feature Creatures workshop at Lone Pine could truly be a menace. I tried to think of the last time I'd seen Aunt Becca or Gabriela. Gabriela had come to one of my openings, a beautiful, quiet girl with more of her dad's Japanese blood showing than my faint hint of the Orient. Aunt Becca...I had no picture of her face in my mind at all.

It lacked a certain sincerity to lament a bond you'd never pursued in the life that came before.

But I still felt guilty as I deliberately let it go.

I stopped to lift my gaze to a spire of iron-red rock spearing a cloudless blue sky. A piece of footage from home, one of the places where I'd taken Grandpa Don walking during the times when the drugs had brought Grandma Anala some peace.

She carries death with her. She's heavy with it.

Who said that? Last night, the doctor. Maybe he was right. But in this tiny moment as my gaze climbed the rock to that limitless sky, I didn't feel heavy, I felt lifted. Lifted by the patience and the foolishness, the laughter and the love of all those I had the privilege of sharing my life with. My life.

I reached over and took my mother's hand, gave it a little squeeze.

She squeezed it back.

Chapter 15

"Hagebak is gone. Anna and Matteo say we need to get moving."

Ben leaned in through the doorway. He, too, was richly re-outfitted in designer jeans, boots, and a fine-striped black and white button-down shirt. Wow. I tossed back the last of my tea and set the cup on the sill.

"I'm ready. Is Ryan going to be able to keep up?"

"We'll have to take it a little easy. The doc thought he'd dislocated it, but it's just strained and bruised up pretty good. He's taped up and drugged. Should be okay in a few days. I'll get him working it once the swelling's down a little more."

I nodded and crossed the small room to where he stood.

"And how are you?" I asked.

"Fine, just need to get movin'. Somethin' tells me the doc left for a reason." He reached for my shoulder, then realized it was uncovered, and circled down to my arm. "What about you, baby?"

I smiled up at him. God, he looked good in that get up! "I'm good. Feeling kinda floaty, though. The doctor didn't leave any food by any chance?"

"Everyone's eating breakfast upstairs."

He turned to lead the way up. I remembered the look on his face from yesterday and reached after him.

"Ben, are you really okay?"

He spared a glance over his shoulder.

"Fuckin' awesome. Let's go."

Shit.

§

Orange juice, apples, sausages, fluffy rolls with a lightly crunchy crust spread with thick, sweet butter. A bowl of creamy yogurt drizzled with honey.

Oh, god.

Reminding myself I had manners, I looked up from the arrangement and acknowledged the members of our expanded ragtag band. Anna made a quick nod, then lowered her head back to eating as Ben settled in beside her. I blinked at the extreme ruddiness left in her cheeks, but let it drop. I turned to the other side of the room just in time to see Matteo jerk his gaze away. My stomach fluttered as I took in those thick, downcast lashes, the way that heavy silk draped from those square shoulders. For a second I could feel the strength of those warm arms wrapped around me. I caught Ryan watching me and shook it off.

You talked to him yet? I asked my former swarm camera operator—though I was pretty sure I knew the answer.

Not yet. As soon as you eat, we're moving to a more secure location. I need to get him with his guard down.

Well, that's not going to happen around me.

Yeah, I can see that.

Seeing that everyone else was nearly done eating, I lowered to the floor and built myself a generous plate. With the first hurried spoonful, I forgot all about Ben's strained face, Matteo's averted gaze and just savored the flavor, the texture of real, live food.

Not until halfway through my plate did I pause to look around. Ben, Ryan, Anna, Matteo, they were all dressed to the nines, balancing plates of gourmet food on their knees here in the ruins of a church tower. I stared at the half sausage on my plate, the crumbs of a Kaiser roll. Money and power. The question was: whose? The Norwegian doctor...or Jürgen?

Or both.

My stomach gave a little twist. I forced my way through the rest of the meal and set the plate to the side. My pack leaned against the wall behind Anna. I grabbed an apple and scooted over to it. The first thing I noticed was the herbal scent of the bag—it had been thoroughly sanitized. The second thing I noticed was the size. Someone had slipped water bottles in the side pockets. I unzipped the main compartment. It was packed with food. I tucked the apple between a box of crackers and a can of sardines.

"I see your fairy godmother visited."

I glanced over to Anna. My eyes widened seeing her up close.

"Lovely, right?" she acknowledged touching her cheek. She looked like she had a full body sunburn. Some of it was even beginning to peel.

"He give you something for that?"

"He did and it's already helping."

"But he said she has to stay out of the water from now on. Or it will kill her." Ben gave her a pointed look.

"That was my third swim this year. Hagebak said I've developed a chemical sensitivity to something in the water. Guess I'll have to bribe someone to transport the groceries from now on."

Third swim. I was already on my second. I glanced down at my hands. I didn't see anything, didn't feel anything. How the hell was she going to manage living in this city and not get that stuff on her? There was a reason almost nobody lived in the coastal towns anymore. The ocean was a condensed soup of everything we'd under-regulated. A splash and you'd be alright as long as you washed up afterward, but a good long soak, a gulp, or an open wound and you'd be hating life.

I flexed my hands. I'd been scraped all to hell. And I was fine.

Anna began stacking plates and cups and I returned to examining the new contents of my pack. I unzipped the top pouch. First aid supplies. I rummaged through them. A bag of powder labeled sanitizer, another powder labeled antiseptic, bandages, a pouch with a needle and what looked like suture thread. Like I was going to be playing surgeon anytime soon. Then my fingers found the smooth glass of a vial. I pulled it out and rolled it over to read the label. Stinger toxin.

A frost crept over the surface of my skin. I jerked my gaze up. This time Matteo stared me down. I tried to hide the bottle, but he'd already seen it, that much I could tell. My lips parted, but his expression only became more serious. He gave a jerk of his head.

Everything inside me tensed with denial. But even as I started to shake my head no, my body remembered being slammed to the floor by tiny little Anna, remembered the ring's knock-out toxin as the only thing that saved me from the murderous wrath Hadria had channeled through her.

Matteo finished shouldering a brand new day pack of his own and took an unrelenting step toward my rebellion. He was right. I knew he was right, but it didn't stop me from hating what my actions said to him as I pulled the vial free of the pocket once more. With a flick of the stinger ring on my finger, I activated the tiny needle and pressed it through the rubber cap of the vial. Once it had drunk its fill, I deactivated it and rotated the ring back to the safety position.

Gritting my teeth, I dropped the vial back into the bag, closed up all the pack's zippers, and flung it over my shoulder as I rose. Matteo still watched me. He gave me an abrupt nod, then turned to follow Ryan out the door, nearly stumbling over Ben in his hurry to get away from me.

The longest eye contact we'd maintained since that fucked up night.

So why did I feel like bursting into tears?

༄

With light from gaps in the church ceiling, Ben and I took one look at Anna's boats and decided to risk the time to better secure them at a level in the rubble above the water marks. Then Matteo took point and we headed back into the ruins through the back of the church.

Our entire group was jumpy like cats before a storm, but the anxiety wasn't reflected in the speed of our progress. Matteo proved a gentler leader than I, but with Ben spotting Ryan through the climbs, my constant stops to regain my equilibrium, and Anna's silent suffering—even the soles of her feet were scalded—we gave the impression of a defeated army returning home in shame.

An hour into the journey I was soaked with sweat and panting.

Where are we, Mo?

She showed me a picture of a circular campo with the Church of the Busty St. Mary at one end and ourselves at a little less than halfway around the perimeter.

"Are you shitting me?!"

I got a chorus of hisses in return and shut my mouth.

Matteo stopped in the midst of ducking into a low hole broken through yet another ravaged wall. He straightened and craned his head around. His eyebrows rose. Great. I looked as shitty as I felt.

"We're almost there," he whispered.

Well, that got color into my cheeks. I nodded. Gestured for him to continue.

But six duck holes in a row later and I didn't dare get to my feet after tumbling through the last. One real meal hadn't repaired that much damage. I sat with my arms wrapped around my knees and my head down, knowing I had to get up and get moving, not sure how to do it without taking a swan dive.

I had the vague impression of a hand wrapping around my arm. Carefully, I raised my head. Matteo was so near. I knew I wanted that, but more than that I couldn't grasp.

"It's just right through this door, Alyse. You can make it."

Reluctantly, I looked away from him, puzzled over an ornately carved door with ivy weaving across it in a swirling, deliberate pattern. Around the door, the wall framed this artistry with the bloated brick and crumbling plaster that had become a blur in my image of Venice.

"Come on, Alyse. I'll help you to your feet."

I wanted to ask him, "What feet?" I couldn't feel any. But he wrapped those arms around me and pulled me into the air and something must have been under me, because his grip wasn't tight enough to support all of my weight.

Clinging to his arm, I stumbled forward, squeezing my eyes closed, then open to keep my vision clear. Matteo reached out and touched the door. Slowly, it swept open before us, revealing only shadows. I hesitated.

Matteo pulled me tighter, whispered into my ear, "This place is protected. They can't reach us, can't control us here. You'll be safe."

But I resisted ever so slightly as he pulled me into that darkness.

Chapter 16

"Who are these people, Matteo?"

"Yeah, dude, who...oh...my...god, dude! It's her! It's, it's her! Oh, my god!"

We emerged from the shadows and I saw the faces attached to the voices. One, a pale woman in her mid-thirties with her dark brown hair pulled into a low ponytail at the nape of her neck and her eyebrows pulled low in an expression of mistrust. The other...the other, a darker, slightly younger man of mixed descent, short and stocky with a face like a five-year-old at Christmas. The woman hung back at the makeshift table while her friend ran forward to greet us.

"Dude, when you said you used to know her, I thought you were shitting me! Ms. Bryant, I am a huge fan of your work. I did one of my college research projects on you. Dude, any chance I could ask you how you did the scene from Calypso Dancing where the dude feels like he's getting tangled in her loom? I mean I tried to pull the file apart and I totally can't figure it out."

Dude, I was the topic of college research projects? Good god.

Exhausted just from the idea of a conversation with the kid, I dropped my head to Matteo's shoulder. The poor kid blushed scarlet. Great, now I was a diva.

"Ernesto," Matteo said, "these guys all had a rough night. Why don't we let Ms. Bryant rest for a few minutes, then I'm sure she'd be happy to answer your questions. Claire-Marie, could you help Anna? She's injured her feet."

With a startled look, Claire-Marie hurried forward and disappeared behind me. Ernesto ducked to the side.

"Hey, man, anything you need me to, like, do?"

"Yeah, can you make sure the bed in my room is set up?"

"Sure." Ernesto hustled off through the doorway ahead of us and Matteo led me along behind.

I looked around me as Matteo ushered me forward. This protected place of theirs had the feel of a thieves' hideout: furniture built from stacks of beams layered over with weathered pillows and tattered lengths of fabric, windows filtering light with chips of colored glass blocking any real view of the lagoon. Jagged patches of multi-colored light on the gray floorboards matched the faded collage of color piled throughout the rooms.

We entered a side room, long and narrow, nearly empty save a bed at the back end and a heavily draped window at the front. Ernesto straightened from flipping a blanket over the bed. He hesitated as Matteo and I lowered to the edge of the mattress, but quickly changed his mind, left the room, and closed the door behind him.

Matteo pulled his arm free of the backpack I wore and we both untangled ourselves from our straps. Each pack hit the creaking floorboards with a riveting thud in the too perfect silence. I kept my gaze to myself in the long stillness that followed. But then I felt him shift to rise. I slipped my hand to his knee. After a moment the resistance of his muscles softened. He wrapped a hand over mine. A rush of toxic tension released out of me at that touch, the rough scrape of his palm across the frail smoothness of the back of my hand sweeping it away.

But even with that connection, the silence continued on too long.

So many questions pricked against my scalp, but I had agreed to let Ryan do the questioning. I grasped after the one I'd hoped was most benign. I didn't want the connection to break. Not yet. Just a second more.

"What is this place? Your hippie artists' retreat?"

Matteo laughed. "Kind of. This used to be the home of Domenico Venier, Ca' Venier. He ran a literary salon here. Veronica Franco was one of the members. I guess it was a pretty big deal—it is to Claire-Marie anyway. We just use it as a sanctuary, a place to pretend the politics out there," he gestured toward the window, "don't exist. And I guess Claire-Marie and Anna have tried to put some color into it."

"Veronica Franco?" I turned my hand over and ran my thumb over the edge of his finger.

"I live, if a person can live / when her soul is wandering, banned," he tried.

I shook my head, not recognizing it.

He tried again.

"I live, if a person can live
when her soul is wandering, banned,
when misery's all she can give
to her faraway lover and land.

I lament the hour and the day
I was torn from my city and lover,
For him, all my bones burn away;
Dry ashes are all I recover.

How lucky you are, blessed Venice,
To hold that man close in your arms!
Without him, I suffer the menace
Of a cold heart that no lover warms."

I was silent, replaying the words in my mind, even as I savored the warmth of his skin against mine. "Torn from my city and lover." "Her soul is wandering, banned." I squeezed his hand, understanding all too clearly how this Veronica Franco's work might have become a theme here in the camp.

"She was...she was Venice's most famous courtesan," Matteo continued, his voice a little sad, a little lost, "but she came here to this place to work on her poetry. Domenico was her patron. Claire-Marie, well, she used to be a lit professor."

Our fingers were intertwined now. I felt his flesh at each juncture of my own. I let my knee fall against his, rested our joined hands against my thigh.

"A poet prostitute?" I raised an eyebrow.

"She was what they called an honest courtesan. She entertained her clients intellectually as well as physically. Apparently, her wit and beauty were just as highly prized as her...other talents."

Everything in me tightened as his hand opened ever so slightly and his fingertips pressed against my inner thigh through the separation of my fingers. His hand slid free from mine and grasped my leg just behind the knee, kneading, pressing. I ran my palm up the flesh of his arm beneath the weighted silk of his rolled up shirtsleeve.

Unrestrained, his hand slipped higher up the inside of my leg. The thin fabric of my leggings made the sensation of his touch that much richer. I arched, one breast pressed into his arm, urging him higher.

Matteo froze, clutching my thigh.

"Alyse."

A remembered panic flashed through me. For a second I froze, too. Then I relaxed my grip on his arm, and took it more fully into my embrace.

"Matteo, it's okay."

That hard grip finally made it to the almost painful ache it had created. I knew he could feel the beat of my blood as he cradled me, digging through the fabric. My womb fluttered and I stretched to press my cheek against his, to seat myself more completely in his grasp. I whimpered, arched, clutched after that hard-muscled arm, the soft tenderness of my breasts wrapping around it completely as I took him more fully to me.

"Alyse," he whispered.

I tugged at the corner of his lips with my own. With an abrupt twist I was in his arms, his lips on mine, forcing my mouth open, forcing me to acknowledge the gaping void within me I wanted him so desperately to fill, a hollowness like a shaft running from my mouth, down my throat, into the pit of me, into my very soul. I wrapped my legs around his hips and we fell to the bed, fitted together so perfectly I lost my breath swallowing his shuddering groan.

And then he was gone.

My senses returned to me slowly. I pressed a hand to my lips, a hand to my lower abdomen, trying to steady myself, trying to slow the sensation of coming undone. My vision still swirled as I propped myself up on my elbows. Matteo perched on the end of the bed, his head in his hands.

"Hey," I tried.

"Alyse, I almost killed you. You would have died, if I hadn't...." His hand drifted to the metal brace on his right arm. He turned to say more, but saw me and his expression changed in the space of an erratic heartbeat. The fire in those eyes. He wanted me. Every part of me. Right down to the essence of me. My breasts throbbed, the space between my legs pulsed. My head dropped back as I tried to collect myself, pull myself back from that dangerous edge.

"I think...I gotta...I'm going to go."

"'Kay," was all I managed as I let myself collapse to the bed. I heard the door close again and buried my face in the pillow to muffle my groan.

But goddamn it, it smelled like him.

∽

I knew I was sleeping.

I could still feel the frustrated hum on my skin, sense the light of day, red through the closed lids of my eyes.

And yet I was trapped in the dream.

I stood amidst the ruffling sheer steel curtains of Jürgen's office, overlooking the flooded St. Mark's Square. I watched the toxic water sway with the wind and the pull of the twilight moon.

How lucky you are, blessed Venice, to hold that man close...
Venice...
Venice...

...to eat with someone else's mouth, to sleep with someone else's eyes, to move according to someone else's desires, clearly running toward the wreckage of your faculties and your life; what misery could be worse?

I knew he stood behind me before his words pressed against my ear.

"*Believe me: among all possible mundane calamities this is the extreme one; but then if we add to the worldly considerations also those relating to the soul, what a perdition and certainty of damnation is this one?*"

I glanced behind me, saw his too-perfect face, cold in its artful symmetry. He drew a lock of my hair back behind my shoulder, leaving his view unobstructed. His hands wrapped around my bare shoulders. It didn't hurt. I was one of them now. Beneath the constriction of the strapless black gown I wore, my heart shuddered, electric.

"Those are her words, Veronica Franco. You can see how her view of the courtesan's life began to change. The greatest and proudest of her profession. *'To give oneself as a prey to many...'* Those are not the words of the girl who once reveled in her hedonistic freedoms." His skin brushed my cheek in the barest ghost of a touch as he spoke.

"Jürgen, I will not turn myself over to you. To you or that woman."

The pressure of his hands slid down my arms, shifted to my waist.

"You won't have a choice." His fingers dug, ever so slightly, into the soft flesh beyond my hipbones. I could not hide the tremor in my breath. "You will come to me or Hadria will break you. She will destroy the pieces of your heart, one-by-one. Innocent victims you have endangered through your pride. She awakens even now. Her servants deliver the news of your survival, the news of your weakness. She will not abide your lack of fealty. Not in her domain. Soon perhaps not even in mine."

His lips grazed my jaw, his hands across my torso pressed me hard against him. The tremble spread from my breath to my body. I saw my breasts shoved high, barely contained above the neckline of my gown. He was taking me apart, unpicking my will thread-by-thread. Terrified, I reached for the open window. It was like plunging my hands into ice. Something was out there. Something deadly. I snatched my hands back. My trembling turned to shaking.

"So long she has slept. She sleeps no more." His lips pressed to my ear. "Come to me, Alyse. Come to me and live."

"No!"

I slammed a heeled shoe down on his foot, drilled an elbow in his ribs. His arms barely loosened enough for me to twist around.

"Let me go!"

I reared back for a head butt, but he recognized the move and leaned out of the way. It gave me enough room to free an arm. I landed a tight left hook square on his jaw.

Jürgen stumbled back. I grabbed up my skirts like some dark Cinderella and ran.

I wrenched the door open before he caught my arm.

"Alyse, she will kill them all and it will all be on you. Don't do this. I am responsible for those people. Please don't put any more deaths on my conscience."

For a moment, as I struggled against his hold, I saw beneath that regal perfection the flicker of a man tired with grief. I snarled at this last of his tricks. With my entire body weight I yanked.

"Let me go!"

He released me.

And I fell through the doorway.

Into the nothingness beyond.

Chapter 17

"Good god, she's strong! Alyse, come on, pull yourself out of there."

"Wake up, baby girl."

I heard the voices through the darkness. Knew them.

Matteo.

Ben.

But those hands that fought to restrain me, I thrashed against them.

"Let me go!"

Then darkness snapped off. I found myself screaming at Matteo as he tried to block my attack. I was curled up on the floor beneath the bedroom's only window. I froze.

"You're back?"

I stared from Matteo to Ben, then saw Ryan beyond them. Ben and Ryan looked terrified. Grafting. They thought I was grafting. I grabbed hold of Matteo's shirt, begged him to believe me.

"Jürgen..."

"I know."

I collapsed against his arm, releasing the tension from my fists, trying to breathe.

"He said she's coming. He said I will get you all killed unless I go back to the palace, back to him." I grabbed the beaten bronze that encased his forearm. "He'll do this to me, won't he? What will this do to me?"

"Put the seven levels of your soul up for auction." Another voice from the back of the room. Claire-Marie.

"That's not true, Claire." That was Anna.

Matteo pulled his arm free from my grip and drew me closer. I dropped my forehead to his chest, stared fixedly at the folds of dusty black fabric at his knee.

"You're not going to have to worry about it, Alyse. You aren't like us. You won't need it to stay sane."

"Dr. Franco said I needed the treatment. He said it would help me. He said I was acting like a stage one patient."

"Dr. Franco doesn't know shit. He has no idea where your patch came from or what the differences mean. For all his supercomputing access, he hasn't come up with jack shit. Not a single theory. Personally, I think this whole thing pushed him off the deep end a long time ago."

I raised my head and straightened.

Nothing? He knows nothing? I asked Ryan frantically.

He'd heard it suggested that your patch was merely from a different Sleeper. All the Brighton's patients received their patches from the Princess.

But it's a long, involved process, isn't it? How could I have a piece of my memory that big missing? Someone *would have to know—you guys, my family...*

Matteo cupped my cheek then and I shifted my gaze to his.

"As for Hadria, she can't come here. None of them can come here."

"But—"

"Jürgen, he's a level six. Has been for years, both him and Suzi. He...he forgets sometimes."

"Forgets what?"

Matteo's gazed slipped briefly to the bronze cuff revealed by his shirt sleeve.

"His humanity."

I remembered that flash of grief on Jürgen's face. *Please don't put any more deaths on my conscience.*

Then Matteo pulled away from me. I looked over and saw Ben pushing him aside.

"Look, sorry, dude, I don't know what you think is going on here, but I've got a real strong suspicion that wasn't no ultra-vivid avatar meeting. Alyse, you need to get running another scan. Make sure everything's still where it belongs in that head of yours."

"Holy shit! You think she's grafting?" Ernesto exclaimed. Our film-making enthusiast strikes again. I saw Matteo's brow wrinkle in confusion and I turned a glare toward Ben.

"I simply think she should run a scan and make sure her gear is still operating properly," Ben said in his best PR voice. Too late for that cover-up, buddy.

"Food first this time, please."

I dug through the layers of curtain at my back and found the wall, used it to push myself to my feet. I found myself looking out into six pairs of eyes.

Always great to have an audience.

Ben reached for my elbow. I shook him off. As I skirted the now awkward group and headed for my backpack, I saw Matteo thread his way toward Ernesto. He would have his answers. I still didn't have mine, not really. I wasn't asking the right questions. I knew I wasn't, but my mind wouldn't stop spinning. I just needed a minute, just needed a second to...

"Alyse." I recognized that there was a hand on my arm. I blinked and turned my head from my pack. Anna crouched next to me. "Claire-Marie and Ernesto have made dinner. Why don't you save that stuff for later?"

I looked down at the boxes and cans in my half-open pack. Nodding, I rose with my Grocery Girl. Together, we followed the others out into the main room, then through a doorway into a dinning area. Ben seated himself protectively beside me. Matteo took the chair at the head of the table. Near enough, but carefully separate.

The chairs were haphazard found things. Mine tottered when I settled onto it; Ben's creaked dangerously. But the food that fogged the chill air over the table had been made with care. Steamed green beans, buttered baby potatoes, homemade bread—only the meat betrayed its prepackaged nature, thinly sliced and piled in a bowl of au jus.

"Thank you for this," Ryan said.

"No, problem, man," Ernesto replied.

Claire-Marie just gave a dignified nod.

The clatter and clank of serving began as the dishes moved back and forth across the table. Ernesto, predictably, launched the conversation with a barrage of questions.

"So are you ever going to do a documentary of, like, your process? I mean, I know Atleiter Productions already did one, but everybody knows you and Bryce knock them outta the park."

Maybe because Bryce and I couldn't be in the same room together? Maybe because I wasn't an actress or a PR mouthpiece as this prolonged silence indicated so very clearly. Where was Tamsin when you needed her?!

I cleared my throat. "It had never really come up." Since Emory wasn't that stupid. "And now it is no longer possible."

"Shit. I mean, dang, I sort of forgot about that. I thought maybe you could sort of build it remotely, you know?"

"Probably best that I keep off the radar for now."

"Ah, yeah."

Awkward silence. Great, Alyse, the Conversation Slayer. I stuffed a forkful of potatoes into my mouth as a lame cover.

Ben kicked my left foot, but came to my rescue anyway. "So, which of the movies is your favorite, Ernesto?"

"Oh, god, well, let's see. I love that loom scene from Calypso Dancing, but the scene from Last Cry where the wolf is running through the woods in the fog and then breaks through to see the moon and she just throws her head back and lets out this howl and it's just the saddest sound in the whole world? That one is just amazing."

I smiled. The kid had good taste.

"That scene is my favorite, too," I admitted.

"I saw this one, as well," Claire-Marie said. "I am wondering how you can make this experience so real when you cannot know the feeling of a wolf."

With a look I tossed the question to Ryan. I was careful with my gaze, though, I could see that Matteo's guard was lowering with the banter and I didn't want to do anything to raise it again. I had questions for him now that my mind had settled a bit. Questions I didn't want Ben and Ryan hearing.

"Tamsin, our field coordinator, did a lot of research to help us understand wolf behavior before we even got started. For that film we did have the wolf trapped and then attached tracking dots for the cameras, so we got some amazing footage and a ton of physical data to feed the computer."

"But truth is," Ben interrupted, "Alyse has got this freakish empathy for animals. I've seen her work. She takes one track from this file about freaking mountain climbing and one track from this ballet bit and a couple other bits and all of sudden she's got you believing you're this wolf leaping up this hillside of boulders. Freakish."

"Yeah, Ben, they got it. Freakish." I smiled over at him and shook my head as I directed his forkful of beans away from my face.

"But, dude, you gotta have millions of hours of sensory footage. How do you even know where to start?" Ernesto demanded.

Standard interview question number three. I tried to keep my answer from sounding too canned.

"Well, I'm pretty familiar with my library, so that helps. When you are putting together the tracks, it's as much about the emotion as it is about physical movement. You have to study the animal, how they move, what their reactions are, then simplify it from what you would experience emotionally—take out the words and the nuances. Then it's just a matter of capturing all that and breaking it down into elements familiar to you and grabbing those from your library."

Anna reached for another slice of bread and Ernesto handed her the crock of butter. Anna's face showed blatant disbelief as she carefully smoothed the butter over the soft bread.

"You make it sound so simple, but I've been to some of your films. I even remember this wolf scene. I don't think anyone who's ever seen it could ever forget it. The films you and Bryce Deacon have worked on...the other houses never even come close. The sensation, the feelings, they just sort of explode inside you as you're watching. You are trying to tell me that's just a matter of programming?"

I stared at her as those soft eyes rose from her work. I hesitated.

"No...all the houses have roughly the same software. Well, I guess we've all made modifications...."

"Many poets put pen to paper. Only some will have the power to let their words continue to echo through time."

I stared at Claire-Marie. Part of me wanted to weep. Part of me wanted to shake my head in denial. Her no-nonsense expression bent with a small, understanding smile.

I cleared my throat as I pushed my plate aside. "So...speaking of poetry, Matteo tells me this place used to host a literary salon?"

I glanced around the tiny dining/kitchen area, more grey than golden. I suspected this *casa* had long ago been converted to apartments.

Claire-Marie dabbed at her mouth with a paper towel as if it were a fine linen.

"What you say is true. This is the salon which hosted Veronica Franco. I once taught her works at the university. You know of her?"

"Only a little."

"There were not so many choices for women in those times. The sixteenth century. After a failed marriage, rather than be a kept woman in a convent, she chose to keep men as clients as her mother did. In this way, she could enjoy financial, social, and intellectual freedoms that wives and nuns could not. In her time, you see, women were not allowed to learn, not allowed to be seen in public. Their power was given entirely to their men. Veronica, she chose a rebel path. She became very famous. The rich merchants, the powerful kings, they all came to her. She reveled in her position, in her power.

"But eventually, the plague came to Venice. Her home was looted in her absence. Much of her wealth was lost. Her children's tutor became angry with her. He accused her of witchcraft before the Inquisition. We suspect this tutor, Redolfo Vannitelli, stole fine things from her home and used the trial to have her killed. He failed. Veronica's speech before the Inquisition was wise and her patrons powerful, but her reputation, it suffered and so did her finances.

"Veronica, she discovered the life of a courtesan also had its traps. This place where we are," Claire-Marie gestured around her with the point of her napkin, "this palazzo was owned by Domenico Venier, her literary mentor and her social shield. With his death, she was left unprotected.

"We have writings from her, warning mothers to steer their daughters away from prostitution, away from dangers and the eternal damnation."

I nodded. I knew those words, they chanted in my mind, blended in the voices of Jürgen and Luciana over and over again: *...to eat with someone else's mouth, to sleep with someone else's eyes, to move according to someone else's desires...* I closed my eyes and pushed the sound away.

"We also have some records of her efforts toward founding *Casa del Soccorso*, a refuge for unwed mothers and other ladies who had lost their...virtue. The children could be safe there while the women worked jobs and were not forced into the life she had known.

"She knew what awaited herself and her children. The money from her time of fame could not support them forever. Unfortunately, she was quite right in this. The city which made her, also unmade her. She died only forty-five years old. She died in the quarter of town reserved for poor prostitutes."

Claire-Marie finished her lecture by placing her napkin just so next to her plate and looking around the room, maybe trying to picture the badly repaired wallpaper as it once had been, filled with gilt furniture and finely dressed men and women with time enough to set together words that would "echo through time."

Matteo, Anna, and Ernesto looked a little glazed, but my two were leaning forward, a little of Claire-Marie's look reflected on their own faces.

"Wow, forty-five? To have all that and then just boom, done?"

I cocked my head at Ben's exclamation, confirmed with Mo.

"You have to remember this is the 1500's we are talking about here," I reminded him. "The average life expectancy was around age 50. I mean, think of all the things you and I would have already died of by our age even. It's more, I think, how far society raised her and how far they dropped her when they got tired of her."

Ryan nodded. "Still happens plenty today."

"Yes, but there is one important difference," Claire-Marie interjected. "Without a man to care for them, these women had no way to survive. The freedoms women like Veronica had enjoyed during their fame, became their chains. The money, it disappeared and because of what they were, the law would not lift a finger to protect them. It was a terrifying way to end a life."

"Geez." Ben rubbed a palm over his clean-shaven scalp, came away with a smear of dirt he tried to discreetly wipe off on his napkin. "So you probably know some of her poetry. Was she any good?"

Claire-Marie smiled wisely. I just raised an eyebrow at Ben. Was he just caught up in the story or did I never know he was into poetry? At all. Ever.

"Hmm, what might you enjoy? Perhaps this one:

        "Then the months and years passed by
so that I had to change my style,

as perhaps you also did.

Now I see you very changed
from what you used to be before,
in the flowering April of your life.

Oh, what a heavenly, angelic countenance
yours was then, able to warm anyone's heart,
even one frozen or as solid as diamonds!

Now, after such a joyful spring,
far more than summer's, you wear autumn's guise,
very different from the first.

And though of a vigorous and manly age,
with the gold of your hair turned to silver,
you appear almost old,

although, in your face, the former light
of noble, calm beauty is not all spent,
and it dazzles whoever dares watch you closely."

Anna nodded. "I like that one. But tell him the one where she challenges that rude man to a joust. 'When we women, too, have weapons and training.' That one."

Claire-Marie chuckled. "Just a little bit, then.

"When we women, too, have weapons and training,
we will be able to prove to all men
that we have hands and feet and hearts like yours;

and though we may be tender and delicate,
some men who are delicate also are strong,
and some, though coarse and rough, are cowards.

Women so far haven't seen this is true;
for if they'd ever resolved to do it,
they'd have been able to fight you to the death.

And to prove to you that I speak the truth,
among so many women I will act first,
setting an example for them all to follow.

On you, who are so savage to us all,
I turn, with whatever weapon you choose,
with the hope and will to throw you to the ground."

Ben threw his head back and roared with laughter.

"Bam! Take you down! Man, she must have been pissed! Though, tryin' to picture her jousting in one of them four-ton dresses kinda ruins the effect."

I raised an eyebrow at my dusty bodyguard, but chuckled despite myself. He looked over at me.

"Hey, dude, my mom was an English teacher before she signed on to tutor Lone Pine's fame-deprived little brats."

I gawked at him. "Please, tell us how you really feel!"

"Hey, you've met them."

"Yeah, and some of them are really well-behaved and professional. *Most* of them."

"That's because you scare them."

"And you don't?"

"Mom don't."

I conceded that one with a tilt of my head. Ben's mom was sweet and adorable.

"Hey, your mom isn't exactly a pushover, man," Ryan interjected as though my concession were offensive. "She's got most of our directors standing at attention and taking orders. Nobody's tried to play it loose with the child labor laws around Lone Pine in decades."

I drop my gaze to my plate with a quiet smirk. I'd have bet money Ryan had a teacher crush on Ben's mom. Big money. He even volunteered at her at-risk kids' afterschool program when we were in town. My smile softened and I raised my head again. There was a good heart behind that baby-face.

Ryan looked at me like I'd just grown a trio of horns.

I chuckled.

Mo announced a message from my favorite swarm camera operator.

Are you about ready to run the scan?

I sighed, drew a few measures of staph lines across the leftover juices on my plate with my fork. *Yes, Daddy.*

Do you know something I don't?

Yes.

Care to share it?

Care to share how Jürgen, the king of technology, had once more somehow hacked my dreams and tried to seduce me into selling my soul? I could still feel his hands over my stomach, my breasts straining against the stiff fabric, his sweet, dizzying breath on my cheek.

I shuddered. I saw a hand reach for me from the corner of my eye and jerked away. When I looked over, I saw Matteo had snatched his hand back. I closed my eyes for a moment.

"I'm sorry. I forget. I'm just not used to...."

I looked up again and Matteo shook his head. "I remember what it was like. You're doing fine."

I ignored the rest of the table and gave him a wan smile.

"I need to go run my tests. Can I help clear the table?"

I rose and piled my fork and knife on my plate.

Claire-Marie waved me away.

"We will clean this. Go tend to yourself."

Awkwardly, I released my plate and backed away from the table.

"Alright, um, thanks."

I hesitated a minute, then left the mess to their capable hands. Left to go tend to myself.

ço

After a little wandering of the common areas, I found a shadowed corner heaped with pillows and settled in. A large velvet-backed pillow escaped the pile as I leaned back. I picked it up and turned it over. I ran my hand over the rough, patterned texture of the needlepoint artwork, a courtyard garden in full bloom, a narrow fountain at its center.

Grandma Anala had tried to rope me into a simple cross-stitch project once. An over-pixilated kitten curled up in a flower bed. She'd been confined to bed by then. I shifted in the pillows, squeezed my eyes shut at the memory, squeezed the pillow to me. She'd finally decided I'd never outgrown my six-year-old wiggles and chased me off. My cheeks flushed and I rubbed my hand over them.

The woman had been dead almost ten years and could still pack me a guilt trip.

I blew out a breath and leaned my head back against the wall. This scan was a waste of an expensive mineral cocktail, but I would never convince Ben and Ryan I wasn't grafting without running it.

I pulled the packet of pills from my pocket and dry swallowed a pair.

Mo, have Margie watch my levels. When they are high enough, go ahead and run the scan.

Acknowledged.

Clutching the pillow, I closed my eyes. Afterimages of Jürgen waited for me there in my private darkness. I forced myself to relax, shook my head to chase him away. He refused to leave. Slowing my breathing, I stared him down in his too perfect majesty.

Mo, can you pull up a publicity shot of Jürgen Phan Mai from before his treatment for Brighton's Disease?

A little shift in the backdrop of my mind's eye and Mo's image flashed before me. Jürgen Phan Mai giving a university commencement speech somewhere. I zoomed in on the image. It drove me nuts when people pulled faces while they were online, but when my eyebrows rose, I didn't stop them. How could this be the same man? He was handsome certainly. He had that almost too much polish that came from absolutely too much money—sculpted hair, tailored business suit, and a skin suit that had likely been tailored as well. But he was just...a man.

I'd dealt with his type ever since I'd received my first Oscar.

I'd never feared for my soul.

All the while grieving for his.

My stomach lurched and I hugged the pillow tighter.

He forgets sometimes.

Forgets what?

His humanity.

Black soulless eyes flashed in my vision. I squeezed my lids, crumpling the image. But I couldn't stop myself from glancing toward the kitchen, trying to reassure myself that the clank and clatter resulted from the simple domesticity and nothing more. I forced my eyes back closed, focused on the light syllabic rhythm of conversation and told my heart there was no need to race. Slowly, the adrenaline drained down.

But this had been what I'd wanted to avoid. My boys surrounded by Sleepers Syndrome carriers, carriers who could flash to feral predators without nearly enough warning.

And they wouldn't even understand what was happening.

You will come to me or Hadria will break you. She will destroy the pieces of your heart, one-by-one. Innocent victims you have endangered through your pride. She awakens even now.

Innocent victims you have endangered...

I jerked myself upright, trying to disrupt the chant that echoed in my skull. Enough. Matteo said she couldn't come here. I was letting Jürgen fuck with my head. I'd be damned if that was happening. I still didn't understand what that man wanted, but the marrow in my bones shrieked that it wasn't for me to enjoy long life and happiness.

I flopped back into the rumpled pile of pillows, forcibly pushed the thought of threat from my mind, purposely snapped my eyes shut. Tomorrow morning I would have enough of my strength back for another round of parkour. At least enough to get them back to the raft.

I thumbed the stinger ring around my finger.

And if it took a little stinger toxin and a call to the coast guard to get them out of this place, I'd have to risk it.

That familiar prickle started under my rib, gently this time. The little nanobots poured out into my system, performing their diagnostics. Dinner had finally settled comfortably in my belly and my limbs loosened with it. I let my head roll to one side, listened to the kitchen banter approach.

Light flickered across my eyelids as my companions passed near me. Their banter turned to murmurs as they settled in around me. Someone brushed my hair from my face. I knew that touch. Matteo. I savored his nearness, drew in the aura of his body heat near my leg.

"I'm going to turn in," Anna told the others.

"Get some rest," Claire-Marie replied amidst the others bidding her goodnight. But it was two pairs of shoes I heard leaving the room. I kept my smile to myself.

Then I groaned as the nanobots dug in as near my brain as they could reach. Matteo wrapped his hand around mine. I released my death grip on the cushion and squeeze back as my system settled. The scan was nearly complete.

"Any chance they just haven't told you what they suspect?" Ryan asked.

"I suppose it's possible, but I was there when Dr. Franco dug through his comparative analysis report. Unless he spent two hours going over a fake report just to fool me, I don't think so."

"We have someone looking into her previous medical history. But Tamsin has been with her from the beginning. I've been with her for seven. I don't think we're going to find anything there. And the rest of the immersion artists were clean?"

"Yep."

"Are you positive you saw reports on all of them?"

"Yeah, pretty sure."

"What about Bryce Deacon?"

The pressure on my hand went slack for just a second.

"I think so."

Margie detected no new irregularities in your central nervous system.

I sat up, opened my eyes to the dimly lit room. I saw Ryan sprawled in a make-shift easy chair. Claire-Marie perched on a pillowed bench next to him below one of their pieced-together stained glass windows. Matteo sat slightly ahead of me, glancing over his shoulder at my resurrection.

Please pass the report to Ben and Ryan.

Acknowledged.

"So..." Matteo hesitated. "Does it tell you right away?"

"Yeah, she said there are no new irregularities."

"That's good, right?" Matteo twisted now to face me and watched my expression warily.

Ryan answered. "That's the best we can do from here. Without a real brain scan and her mechanic, we're only guessing. But after that last episode and your other footage, I'm inclined to believe something's been knocked loose in there, Alyse."

"I'm fine, Ryan. But it's time for you and Ben to go. There's nothing to find here. Maybe your friend Booth might have some ideas. The four bodies, the ATF has to have some theories about where they went. It wasn't the good guys that ran off with them. At least not from what I've heard."

Ryan watched me for a long, quiet time. The mind behind that baby face had gone hard and sharp.

"Before you even think it," I warned, "I'm staying. I won't risk even one more Haylee landing in a Children's Castle. Not without knowing how this happened. Not without knowing if I can cause the same curse."

"I wouldn't ask it." But I could tell he'd been thinking it, thinking how the ATF could run a medical analysis far more accurately than a worn out Dr. Frankenstein in a rundown castle in the Adriatic. "But I will ask your permission to contact Booth from here." Beside him, Claire-Marie straightened and Matteo even froze just a little bit.

"That is dangerous," he warned.

"You will need the satellites. Jürgen will know everything you say," Claire-Marie agreed.

"And Flaming Sword and The Seers have high-jacked our communications about a hundred times before. You would be putting a lot of people on the outside at risk. Most especially Alyse's family."

"There's always a risk, even with a secure line, but ATF has the best. I would have him contact me and bring him up to speed. See if he can find out anything before Ben and I leave that might help."

I swore I could feel my sternum rattling as my heart smacked against it. Risk my mother, my Uncle Keats, my Aunt Becca and her family, my Grandma Sam? I wanted to tell him I'd sleep on it, that I'd have an epiphany by morning, but in the pit of my stomach, I knew better.

"No."

Only I would have seen the slight sag to Ryan's shoulders, but I couldn't find it in myself to feel guilty. That simply wasn't an option. Especially because from that same pit in my stomach came sibilant whispers that the risk would bring no gain.

"Are you sure?"

"Completely. Whatever I did to cause this, I won't have it coming down on my family—especially when they are already grieving the loss of a husband and brother. I've talked to my mother, Ryan. She's not okay...." I took a second to shove my own grief back, far away from my voice and my face, where it could only sour my stomach instead, "She's not okay and I can't even be there for her. I can't even be there for her."

"That's not your fault, 'Lyse," Ryan murmured.

"It's not? Really? 'Cause I didn't charge off to do an enactment the second she got into town? One way or another, we both know it's my fault. Look, talk to Booth when you get out, but keep it live and off the record. Whatever we could have done here, we tried and we blew it. Doesn't stop you from working on it out there. I'll help how I can."

Ryan leaned forward, his elbows on his knees, his hands clasped. He wasn't ready to give up, but he said nothing. What could he say?

I glanced toward the colored-glass collage on the window. It had lost its shine. The sun was gone. I sat up and gave my friend a sad smile. "Go rest. Tomorrow I will lead you back to the Gesuiti."

And finally send you home.

Ryan nodded as he rose, but those gears still turned behind that watchful countenance. I'd bet by morning he'd have a new argument, a new reason to linger, a new reason not to leave me. I couldn't let that happen anymore. That I already knew. As kind as Ernesto, Claire-Marie, Anna, and Matteo had been to us, that could all change in an instant. This peaceful interlude was more dangerous than my friend could possibly comprehend.

As Ryan bid us goodnight, Claire-Marie rose as well.

"I will take my rest also," she announced. "You have made a wise decision. I will help you in the morning. You will need a hearty breakfast for that journey." Then she turned and followed Ryan toward the other side of the apartment before turning into one of the rooms and closing the door behind her.

I listened to Ryan's boots threaten the patched flooring, listened until I heard that scrape and click of the door one last time.

And finally send you home.

Chapter 18

He walked me to the room. My hyper-awareness of my gait, of the swing of my arms became awkward alongside his absolute caution not to touch me. Holding my hand was obviously only permitted when he thought me unconscious.

I stopped several paces back from the door. He stepped forward, released it, and pushed it open for me. I hurried forward to catch it before it could fall again. With a silent sigh, I held the door for him as he entered. My eyes stayed trained on the grain of the wood as I walked the door closed once more. I listened to the pops and clicks of the simple machine as I slowly released the sculptured glass knob, sealing us inside.

Staring down at the cloudy ornament, I worked up my courage. I turned. He watched me again with those haunted, wary eyes, but there was hunger there now, too, and it brought a beautiful ache low in my belly.

I risked reaching out to him.

His fingertips touched mine, our two hands intertwined. We watched our interlaced fingers as though we had reached each other across some ancient, mysterious divide, both dangerous and divine.

"That night..."

"Alyse—"

"No." I snapped my eyes up to his. "That's not..." I lost myself, just for a second. The depth of those brown eyes. The kindness I remembered, flooding them. "That's not.... For a night you were my magic, Matteo. You danced with me. Remembering home through your eyes, you...." My hand trembled in his as my words tumbled to a halt. How could I make him understand? "On the rooftop, wearing your jacket, holding your hand...you brought me more peace than I've had in years. And then you touched me."

I closed my eyes and shook my head. The words, they weren't working.

His hand clasped mine with a comforting firmness.

"You were home and hope and a taste of freedom," he murmured. "I could imagine I lived in the heart of an empire instead of this moldy, rat-infested prison. That I destroyed that...that I destroyed your life with it...."

I opened my eyes, raised my gaze to his. Now I returned that firm clasp.

"You don't know that. I don't believe that."

I gave up with the words, poured my soul into my eyes, into him. If there was any way to make him understand. I needed that magic back. I needed him back.

I reached up and drew the tear-shaped pendant from my shirt.

Matteo stared in shock at the place on my breast where I lay it to rest. His gaze lifted uncertainly to mine. Then slowly, slowly, I saw what I needed to see. Both gentle and fierce, his own soul rose up to answer mine.

The magic returned.

"You still have the ring?"

I showed him my other hand. He nodded. I lowered it.

Fingers still locked together, he turned over my palm. The moisture of his lips brushed over it, his breath chilled the imprint, sending a shiver down my arm, across that beautiful ache in my belly.

This. This was what I remembered.

Matteo followed that shiver with his lips over the inside of my arm and I closed my lips over a groan. That ache spread, filling my breasts until my bra felt too tight around them. I released his hand and pulled the tunic up over my head, tossing it to the side.

I went to him.

First just a brush of the lips, gently begging for permission, the cool, crisp press of his shirt against my naked flesh sending a tremble through my breath. My fingers wove through the heavy satin of his hair.

He acquiesced.

Those long, strong hands came around my waist and I grew dizzy—just to feel the warmth of someone else's skin against mine. God. I let my head fall back with a moan. My Venetian understood and released me with a flick of the clasp. I freed myself from the straps. He pulled my hips against his. I shuddered, sending my breasts shaking beneath the nearness of his mouth. This is what I wanted. I wanted him inside me, over me, wrapped around me. I wanted his skin on mine.

I wanted it to the point of pain.

I clutched at his shirtsleeves; he clutched at my breast, let the nipple escape to the pinch between his knuckles. Then he began to knead. He pulled until he tugged at the root of my breast, kept that nipple trapped and lifted even higher. I begged without words, sought him mindlessly with limp hands. He switched to the other breast. My begging turned to cries.

He didn't release me.

He ground the hard ridge of his erection against me through the thin fabric of my leggings. I cried out. He yanked me up to smother the sound with his mouth.

I tried to kiss him back, tried to grab hold of him, but my head spun so bad. He backed me toward the bed and let me fall down to it. The rustle of the air flipped locks of hair across my face; the ancient mattress thumped against my back, jostling my sensitized breasts. I bit my lip on a gasp.

Those hands released me from the rest of my clothes. Those eyes released me from my mind. Naked, I reached for him, pulled myself back up to standing with the front of his shirt. I flipped my hair back from my face. He grabbed it, kept my head pinned back with it, kept my body arched with it.

Mine.

From that contorted position, he assaulted my mouth. I assaulted the barrier between us. I found the buttons of his shirt, fumbled my way down them. I parted that fabric and pressed myself against him.

I nearly sobbed. So long, so alone.

"Matteo."

"God, Alyse. Alyse, I've gotta get inside you. God, if you could see the way you look right now."

I could only see on his face the way I looked, only feel what that look sent back to me, the pulse of need that ran from my over-stretched throat in a spiral that left me throbbing at the hollow emptiness exposed by my upturned ass. I gave his belt a yank and he took the cue, shucking the rest of his clothes one-handed, the other hand keeping me tight against him. But as he shook himself free of the last of it, I turned us. When we fell to the bed this time, I was on top of him.

It didn't matter. He wrapped one hand around my breast and yanked me up to suckle me like a starving babe. My ass was left high and open to the chill night air.

But not for long.

First one, then two fingers forced their way inside me, spread me wide.

"Matteo!" I sobbed. My shudders just made the sensation of being opened that much more violently electric.

How could I want him this much after only a few days?

It was insane.

I was insane.

I wanted more.

Now.

I slipped a hand between us, but I couldn't reach him. I tried to force my hips down toward him, but that just opened me wider. The hand at my breast jerked me to the side and he filled his mouth with my other breast, clinging with his teeth, bobbing his head as he suckled, rolling my nipple with his tongue.

"Matteo, I...I...oh, god!"

The electric shards exploded between my thighs, driving up through my abdomen to the tips of my battered and swollen nipples, tearing down through my thighs, calves, to the tips of my toes. My body convulsed around his hand, bucked against his torso.

He released me.

He flipped us over.

He drove himself into me.

I screamed as he pinned my shoulders down and rammed his way into my spasming body. I thrashed, met him with each thrust. He kept that orgasm ripping through me over and over and over, one nipple, then the other, then a thumb to my clit, and I knew that my body had not yet finished coming apart. My arms and legs flung open, even my mouth and throat spread. I wanted him to fill me, to tear me open and fill every part of me.

"Please," I begged. "More, please!"

Impossibly we began to move faster. He pressed my nipples together, drew them both into his mouth.

For a split second that openness collapsed.

And then it detonated.

He let my nipples flip free from his suction, grabbed my hips and plunged harder and harder and harder. A moment later, he snarled and went rigid against my opening, the only motion between us, the pulsing warmth of his seed pumping into me.

We stayed like that until my over-stimulated body began to tremble. Slowly, gently, he lowered us to the damp mattress. We came unjoined, but he pulled me tightly to him, absorbing my shaking, stroking my hair, my stomach, my thigh, kissing the side of my face.

"You're okay. It's okay. I've got you. You're okay, Alyse."

I twisted around and kissed him between shuddering gasps, between aftershocks of the most violent orgasm of my life. He wrapped himself around me, held me together as I held him. My eyes stayed blind, my head still spun, and at the edge of my darkness, something wild and primal licked at the edges of me. My soul reached for it, even as I shrank back in fear: my shark god's chaos, that place of creation and destruction, that place of secret answers, it pulled at me.

"Matteo," I whispered desperately.

"I know, I've got you. Stay with me, Alyse. Hold onto me."

I tightened my hold; he shifted a hand to my face.

"Look at me, Alyse." I turned my head. "No, see me, Alyse."

"I want it, Matteo."

"You aren't ready. Look at me, Alyse. Come on."

I forced my eyes to focus, forced myself to ignore that rending sense of loss as I shut out that chance for knowing, that chance for becoming something greater. The strange grief settled in my chest, but I raised my hand to his cheek, trained everything in me on that soft, sad gaze.

"You are okay this time. Is this...." I had no word for it, so I simply didn't use one. "Is this what happened to you last time? Was I...?"

Matteo pulled me forward and pressed a kiss to my forehead, then ducked down again to look into my eyes.

"No, I don't think you are like us, Alyse." He pulled his left arm from beneath me and I realized for the first time, the metal from his vambrace had cut into the skin of my ribs. I ignored it. "Most of us use this," he paused, shifting to prop himself up on his elbow and reached over our heads to switch on a small reading light. I rolled onto my back to get a better look. "Most of us use this to control the progress of the disease. We have to have help to get through the transitions or we lose it. What you felt just now, we don't see that until level four or five. And if we don't pull back? Some have died. Some just went crazy."

I raised an eyebrow, but I believed him. I'd felt that threat to my sanity and clinging to my will to resist had been a terrifyingly tenuous thing.

"I will try to be careful," I promised, but the memory dance in my head, nipping, taunting with just as much threat and menace as Jürgen's relentless stalking.

"Alyse, hey."

I jerked my eyes back from the darkness, my mind back from the looping nightmares.

"Let it go. Just for a few minutes, you have to let it go. All of it." Matteo stroked my hair back from my face. I took the chance to trace the lines of his bicep, the rises and falls intriguing beneath my fingertips. Slowly, he lowered back down to prop his head on his hand. In the amber light, he traced my collarbone with his fingertip, arranged his tear-shaped pendant in the hollow of my throat.

"You are so beautiful. Your body, the way you move. When you were gone.... When you were gone, you were in my dreams almost every night. Sometimes you were screaming at me for what I'd done. Sometimes you were above me, teasing me with these breasts." He blew at the reddened nipples and drew them to peaks with the stroke of his fingers. My back arched and he blew at them again, smoothing his hand down my stomach.

"Sometimes you rode me with this." His hand slipped between my legs, his two fingers sliding right inside me, wriggling, probing. I gasped and bucked. "You rode me with this until I was screaming." He sat up and spread me open wide, latched onto my clit with his teeth and played at it with his tongue, ignoring my struggles, ignoring my pleas until I was the one screaming.

Too much!

I reached for his head; he reached for my breast and began strumming the swollen nipple. Then he grabbed my breast at the base, shaking it roughly. My already swollen nipple became engorged with sensation. I strained just to breathe. Never releasing my clit, he curled me forward, so he could reach my other breast, shaking it until it, too, was red from the violence, until it throbbed with too much feeling. He released it.

I watched him shift to wrap an arm around my upraised hips. I watched him shift so that he could watch me as he separated the two fingers inside of me to spread me wide. I watched him shift so he could watch me as he lapped and sucked at my clit, his tongue teasing the edge of my opening.

He breathed into me.

I swore I felt that chill run up through the center of me, through my lungs, my shuddering breasts, then out my own mouth.

"Matteo! You, I....please!"

"Let it go, Alyse. Just for a minute, let it all go."

He lowered his head. I screamed. I pressed my palms to my own nipples, feeling the pulsing heat there. I tried to buck, but his teeth, his metal-sheathed arm trapped me.

"Open your eyes, Alyse."

I obeyed, not remembering closing them.

"I want to see you come."

Then he lifted his head. I watched that one, long finger slide into me. My hands spasmed over my breasts. Then that finger twisted and found what it was looking for. It played and cajoled; I flailed. A thumb rose to my clit and opened it up. Inside and out I was stroked, so raw, so desperate, so painfully frantic.

"Open your eyes, Alyse."

"I can't!"

"Open your eyes, Alsye."

My eyes flew open. I saw him there, his long hair sweeping my wide-splayed thighs as he held me open and dug into me with his tongue. Dug and dug and dug. My wide-splayed fingers clenched around my nipples. Harder, harder, harder!

Matteo's teeth scraped up my clit.

Two fingers rammed into me.

The spasms choked off my scream.

My body whipped into a rigid arch.

He didn't miss a beat, working me through the spasms, through that final rending until my muscles went lax and he lowered me to the mattress, even then keeping a gentle rhythm until he slowly slid his fingers free and raised his head.

"Sleep now, Alyse. Let it all go."

The blanket brushed over my skin as he drew it over us. His touch brushed over me, gently soothing until I felt it no more.

Chapter 19

Matteo was dreaming.

I could feel him shifting restlessly at my back. I rolled toward him, draped my chill body over him. Beneath my arm, my breast, my hip, my leg, his muscles stilled, relaxed. I smoothed my palm across the rises and falls of his chest, savoring the feeling of his satin humanity beneath my palm, not wanting to wake him.

And yet not wanting to be without him while he slept.

The space between my legs throbbed now with pain. My breasts protested the contact I forced upon them. But I would have ignored it all to be so perfectly joined with him just one more time.

I felt my eyes tearing and knew it was an overdose of hormones coupled with an overdose of exhaustion, but I curled closer anyway. I drew my hand away from Matteo and ran it over the lowest part of my own abdomen.

The permitted pair.

The two little sparks of life the law would have allowed to quicken in my womb. The two little sparks of life I would never have. So much to give up. A little girl to take shopping at Aladin's with Tamsin and Mom. A big brother to boss her around, to sneak her cookies when he thought Ben wasn't watching. Two little bodies to hold close during the scary part of the story at bonfire. Two little faces to light up when Ryan demonstrated his latest Double-O Seven invention. Two little lights to go out when I packed up for another enactment.

I rebelled against the judgment.

I had so much footage already. I wouldn't have to leave them often. A lot of parents had to do some traveling to keep their jobs.

Matteo began to stir again.

With a sigh, I relaxed back against him. Who the fuck was I kidding? Ryan's niece Haylee was the closest thing to a daughter I would ever have now. Her virtual hand was the only tiny six-year-old hand I would ever hold.

The tears started in earnest now.

Such a goddamn hypocrite. Like I'd ever given any serious thought to kids before I got my goddamn ass infected!

Matteo groaned and his head shifted ever so slightly back and forth. Scooting up to reach, I pressed my cheek to his, kissed my tears from his skin.

"Hey, it's okay. Hey."

I pressed kisses up the side of his face, cradled his head against my chest. He had so many more nightmares to haunt him than my petty never-would-be's.

"Matteo, hey, you're okay. Come on, you're okay."

His face crumpled and he tried to jerk away from me. I dropped the whispers.

"Matteo, wake up," I demanded.

His thrashing got worse. I sat up and shook him.

"Matteo!"

That beautiful body arched back with a scream.

And then I knew he wasn't dreaming. Right before he grabbed me and flipped me under him. His teeth were bared in a snarl inches from my face. His eyes lay in shadow, but I knew, I knew they flashed black.

"Matteo." My voice was calm. I silenced any trembling from my body.

"She shouldn't be able to reach us here. How can she reach us here?!" Those long fingers became hooked claws in my wrists. I should have been crying out from the pain.

"Who?"

"Hadria, she's awake. She's too strong. Get out, Alyse! You have to get out!"

"You have to let go, Matteo. I can't move."

That snarl, that heart-stopping predatory cry was my only reply. *Oh, shit.*

And then I *was* moving. I was flying. Across the room until my naked body slammed into the brick of the wall. I took the brunt of it on my shoulder and hip before I crashed to the floor.

Ryan and Ben. *Oh, god, I've got to get to them.*

I could hear low voices beyond the door.

But Matteo was on me before I could get my stunned limbs to push me all the way upright. I redirected his punch with a limp block and spun away.

Mo, tell the boys to get out!

Matteo lunged after me with a feline grace, terrifyingly beautiful in the moonlight. I only just managed to twist out of his way, but my cold foot didn't catch me quite right. I rolled when I hit the floor, felt a sliver of my skin hook on something, then tear away. My feet, I had to get to my feet!

I shoved myself from the floor with everything I had left. I found myself face-to-face with those soulless eyes.

"Alyse, everything okay in there?"

My gaze flashed over Matteo's shoulder to the door. Ryan, you stupid, son-of-a—

Gravity released me. I floated; then he body-slammed me to the floor. For a second my eyes and my ears flicked off as the shock exploded through my ribcage and my head. Wildly, I scrambled to get my left arm free. He shifted his pin, trapping half my hand under my ass. He cocked his arm for a punch. I bucked hard enough to unbalance him, but I lost flesh as I ripped my hand free.

I drove the ring's stinger between his ribs.

I saw the surprise, the confusion.

Matteo collapsed.

The force of his landing cleared the rest of the breath from my lungs; the sharp sting of a bruise blossomed where his cheekbone had hit mine. I chased after my breath in fruitless fits and trips until I was shoving at him frantically. I had to get out!

Sweat had our bodies clinging to one another and the panic I'd kept so carefully under control burst free. I pushed and kicked and twisted like a wild thing, knowing that panicking was the stupidest thing I could do, but not able to hold it back anymore.

A vile smell smothered my senses, a cold hand pressed against my superheated shoulder.

Luciana.

"Does he live, our little Matti?"

I nodded sharply, showed her the ring on my hand.

Satisfied, she rounded me with her tottering gait, grabbed his arm, and pulled. Matteo's dead weight rolled away from me and I scrambled to all fours. Full breaths sent my rib screaming. I ignored it.

Luciana shoved my clothes at me.

"The Huntress comes with the mad mood, little Alyse. Time to ride, time to hide."

That's when I noticed the silence.

I jarred myself into motion. Tears streamed down my face as I forced damaged muscles and joints into instant obedience, jamming my arms and legs into clothes and shoes. Luciana dragged the bag to me.

"More magic for your ring in here? Somewhere inside?"

Even as my ears strained for any signs of life outside the door, I knew she was right. Without the ring, I couldn't help them. I was just so much cannon fodder.

I tore into the upper pocket, clenched the muscles in my arms to slow down the shakes. If I ended up stabbing myself with the damn ring, this show would be over in the space of two heartbeats.

But I got the stinger into the vial and pressed my arms against my knees to keep the connection until the stinger had drunk its fill. I disengaged the ring and shoved everything back into the pack.

With a blanket yanked from the bed, I crossed the room to where Matteo lay sprawled across the floor. Gingerly, I covered him with it. His face, so peaceful, in drug-induced slumber, gave my heart a sharp twist. So fucked up.

I swear to god, whoever this Hadria chick is, she'll wish she'd never lived!

I turned away.

The icy-electric rage sliced through the searing hot pain in my arms, my legs, my torso. My lips peeled back as I stalked toward the door.

And froze.

No, no, no.

I breathed it away, far away. I would find a way to right this, but not by becoming one of those feral nightmares. Checking myself, I swung the pack securely onto both shoulders and joined the formless, faceless shape of Luciana at the door. Silently, we listened. I used that second of silence to finish schooling my nerves. Then I reached out and slowly, so slowly unlatched the door. Who knew the mechanics of a door handle could be so loud?

The door swung open with the appropriate squeal.

One second, two seconds.

Nothing sprang out at us.

One step, two steps heralded my entrance into the empty common room. Somehow Luciana's weight held far less musicality. Which left the spaces between my steps for me to hear the chant:

"He who has lost his body, and he his shadow,
he who escapes himself and he who hunts himself"

The professor. Claire-Marie's voice held a precise beat, a rhythm so focused, I could almost feel her rocking to it. The murmur came from the kitchen.

"who pursues himself and never finds himself, all those,
the living corpses on the edge of the moment,
wait suspended. Time itself in doubt,
day hesitates."

She knew I was coming, the control in her voice grew more desperate, louder, more demanding of her remaining sanity as I reached the kitchen doorway.

"Moving in dream,
upon her bed of mire and water, Venice
opens her eyes and remembers: canopies,
and a high soaring that has turned to stone!"

Holding a hand up to Luciana, I stretched my head very slowly around the doorframe. Centimeter by centimeter, the roughened wood revealed the portrait. Ryan crouched frozen in the far corner past the overturned table and splintered chairs. Blood covered one side of his face, his wide eyes focused on a point just beyond my view. Fuck! How the hell was I going to get him out of there?

"Splendor flooded over...
The bronze horses of San Marco
pass wavering architecture,"

Another few centimeters. Two meters from where I stood, Claire-Marie crouched over Ernesto, pinning him to the floor, rocking in time with her words. I'd seen this before, Anna in the space between human and feral, fighting it so hard, but with the strength and violence to keep Ernesto at bay for at least a few minutes. Frantically, I waved Ryan forward.

He didn't see me.

Mo, tell him to get over here. Tell him to move slow.

Would he even take the message?

An eternity I stared at him in the dim light, willing him to look over. There. His face took on a new expression. He risked a quick glance in our direction. I waved him over like a mad thing. He shifted to a crouch. I motioned for him to keep down. He replied with a short nod.

I kept my focus on Claire-Marie as I waved Ryan forward. I catalogued every detail, the rhythm of her rocking; Ernesto's lack of movement. The heightening arc of her back, the tightening of her voice.

"go down in their green darkness to the water
and throw themselves in the sea, toward Byzantium."

And then my gaze was jerked away.

Ryan scrambled the last half meter to the door.

toward Byzantium...

Claire-Marie.

I snapped my head back just in time to see her spin toward me, her crouch predatory. Her eyes black.

I grabbed Ryan's shirt and shoved him past me just as the professor sprang. I checked her with a shoulder to the ribs. Stupid. She got her claws into my sides. I muffled my own scream and slammed her into the pantry door. That didn't slow her down. Teeth, claws, knees, she drove pain into me from every direction. I ducked and shoved her against the door again, giving myself just enough time to free my left hand.

I drilled the stinger into her thigh.

Hesitation.

She dropped.

She still had a handful of my hair. I came down with her.

I jerked at my hair, twice, three times. Finally managed to free myself from the loom of her fingers. I scrambled back from our two hosts. They didn't move. Ernesto was so completely still. He could be dead. Shit.

Clutching my torn scalp, I lurched to my feet and stumbled to the doorway.

It lay empty.

Oh, god.

Anna.

I sprinted to the end of the hall. The common area was empty save for a glow light behind one of the chairs in the far corner. I heard sounds. I shot across the room. At the edge of the faint glow, I swung off my pack and pulled out the vial of toxin. I shoved the stinger through the rubber cap, tried to breathe through my enforced pause. I couldn't see enough detail to know if the fluid level had stopped moving. It would have to be good enough.

I crammed the vial back in my pack, jerked the bag over my shoulders, and darted toward the hall where the other rooms lay. Claire-Marie's door sat open; Ryan's, too. I couldn't see Anna's, but I heard movement. Keeping close to the shadows of the wall, I slipped forward.

Something moved.

In the pitch dark the plank beneath my foot dipped counter to my step.

I bent my knees and braced myself.

The movement stopped.

Beyond the walls of the apartment, I heard that feral hunting call. An answer. Another answer. Then another.

Even if I got them out of here, where would we go?

Mo, ask Ryan where he is.

Would he even—

Scrabbling in the pitch dark. Shit! I shot forward blindly.

And caught a huge, naked chest in the face.

Human. The fire of skin-to-skin contact tore across my right eye and cheek, down my neck. "Ben?" I hissed.

"Alyse?"

The smell of Luciana hit me full force. Her hard little hand pulled me free from Ben. I limped after her. When we reached the common room, I glanced behind. Ryan followed with their two packs, Ben with his clothes and boots clutched to his full-frontal glory. They were okay. God, they were okay.

Luciana stopped us in front of a shallow coat closet near the front door. As she opened it and started pulling at floor boards, I grabbed Ben's clothes and started handing him pieces. He wouldn't have a single scrap of hide left if he went through one of these Venetian obstacle courses naked.

"Down the hole, down, down beneath the apple tree," Luciana whispered.

I waved Ryan forward as I handed Ben his boots. Luciana lowered her skittering body down the hole. Ryan dropped Ben's pack at my feet and headed for the closet, pulling his own off before he squeezed himself through behind her. His pack disappeared down the side. I tossed Ben his shirt.

"Go!"

He pulled the shirt on and paused only long enough for a single button. Then he grabbed his pack and hurried after Ryan. I was right behind him. As soon as his pack cleared the hole, I rushed into the closet. I made a note of where Luciana stacked the floorboards, set my pack down on the opposite side. Reaching for the door, I caught one last glimpse of Matteo's room, one last glimpse of that long, beautiful hand lying limp on the floor.

This place is protected. You'll be safe here.

Goddamn it!

Shaking my head against the sting of tears, I pulled the door closed behind me.

Chapter 20

I fell.

I fell and nothing caught me.

In the unreality of utter dark there was no up or down. Only the arctic wind streaming my hair back from my face told me I was even still upright.

I was going to hit.

I didn't want to.

Something dragged at my pack in the hand above me.

Something scraped at my shoe.

My shoe, then my ankle. My thigh and my ass hit. I was sliding. Brick? It crumbled powder into my nostrils. I heard muffled exclamations in front of me. I hit a tiny ridge. My leggings were useless against it. I muffled my own exclamation. The ride grew rougher and I reached out, trying to slow myself. Any second now I would plow—

—right into Ben.

I knocked us both face-first into solid darkness. There was no clear air here. I pictured it red with brick powder. I pictured it filling my lungs. I coughed so hard my lungs started spasming. I heard the others doing the same. I tried to climb free of Ben's back. Nothing in that solid darkness that I grabbed held still.

A small, hard hand seized my arm. It didn't hurt. Luciana. I could barely smell her through the dirt. It didn't hurt. Was she one of them? But...but I thought the Venetians were already here....

Luciana pulled me forward until I was steady on all fours. I sat up. Rapped my head. Sank back down. I shimmied my way into my pack. It just barely fit beneath the low ceiling.

Someone tugged at my shirt sleeve. Ben, I knew, because he caught part of my arm. In my fight for air, I no longer cared about the pain. It simply helped wash the earth from my eyes. Blindly, I followed him forward.

The air grew freer, colder. I gritted my teeth against the chill. My mind slipped. Just for a second. It remembered the building collapsing in the canal. It remembered the countless layers of unstable architecture above me. My mind created the weight of fallen stone on my back, crushing the air from my struggling lungs, crushing my bones, crushing my life. My lungs strained against my imagined death; the image of my lost body buried under the rock, burned vivid against a backdrop of impenetrable blackness. Unknown. Forgotten.

It is said that the remains of Marco Polo's Mongol princess bride, Hao Dong, were found beneath the family palace in just such an arrangement.

Fucking lovely, Mo. Maybe we'll hook up with her down here. That'd be awesome.

Unlikely. She is said to wander the rooftops carrying a blue flame, singing in her legendary voice of her love for her lost husband. Though she followed Marco throughout China on his travels, upon their return, Venetian society turned her into a recluse with their contempt for her foreign look and custom. Upon Marco's imprisonment in Genoa, presumably over his non-Christian marriage, his sister Lucia even stooped so low as to tell the lady her husband was dead. In her grief and despair, Hao Dong lit her clothes on fire and threw herself from the palace window into the canal below.

Seriously?

Unlikely. Marco Polo is documented as having married a well-to-do Venetian woman Donata Badoer and having produced three daughters, Fantina, Bellela and Moreta.

Oh.

I cracked a smile at my own stupidity and noticed that the steel band around my lungs had cracked as well.

Thank you, Mo.

You're welcome.

My hand landed on something that wasn't crushed brick. It slid and my arm went out from under me. Ben's shoe, I realized as I headbutted him in the ass. We had stopped. Without the shrill grind of the brick, I heard the wind. And the hunting calls that came with it. Ben shivered under my steadying hand on his calf.

Suddenly, the wind snapped against us. A hint of moonlight cast shadows, interrupting the uniform dark. Luciana had opened a doorway. My teeth rattled. A detriment of being in top physical condition: insufficient body fat for Adriatic winters.

Our wagon train began moving once more. We emerged into the moonlight.

"Son of a bitch!" Ben whispered as the strong frigid wind bit into us.

"More than the winter rides this wind tonight."

In the cold whip of the wind, I felt it, too, the ecstatic wildness, the predatory thrill: Hadria. The Huntress rode with the mad moon. Whoever in the fuck that was.

I squeezed my way out onto the balcony with the others. A balcony which was a mere meter above the water level. I scanned the sliver of sky between buildings, but the moon hid behind the rooftops. We stayed crouched in the shadows, my knees stinging in the wind. But that couldn't matter. The vast ruined city stretched out in my mind's eye.

And hours to go before I sleep.

And hours to go before I sleep.

Chapter 21

I woke up in the grey light of afternoon.

I sat up in my sleeping bag. My left shoulder couldn't bear my weight. My knees would not bend. My ribs would not permit a deep breath. Gingerly, I snagged my pack and pulled it closer. I pulled out a crushed apple, an energy bar, and my vitamins. A water bottle had been set nearby. With excruciating caution I chewed; I swallowed.

I laid back down.

Mo, run Margie when you are ready.

Acknowledged.

☙

I awoke again.

Afternoon had passed. My limbs pulled me easily from the sleeping bag. I turned to face Ryan and Ben. Ryan stirred at the sound. That baby face was coated in red dirt, the left side caked in blood. In my memories, that face grinned as it predicted James Bond's pick up line to the second. That face furrowed in concentration as it tracked a replacement camera into the swarm of our beloved wolf. That face pleaded with me not to lower myself into that shark tank so many days ago.

Beyond him, Ben shot awake. My Ben, my constant companion these last six years. But instead of the crinkle of good-natured teasing, or the hard line of a well-deserved lecture, terror filled those eyes. I crawled over to him.

"She...her eyes, Alyse."

I laid a hand on his shoulder. "I know. I'm sorry, Ben. I was stupid. I thought we would be safe there. I'm sorry."

I heard Ryan sit up behind me. I turned around.

Just in time to see him collapse back to the floor.

"I didn't believe you. I thought you were grafting. It's me who should be sorry," he murmured in a slur.

That slur set my heart to beating. I scrambled back for my pack and settled down beside him. I pulled out one of the bath wipes. Folding it carefully, I began to clean his face. He didn't move, just lay there with his eyes closed.

"You couldn't have known," I murmured. "Psycho-carriers weren't part of the data-set you had to work with."

"The guy fucking tried to kill me. He would have, too, if Claire-Marie hadn't shown up. He was so strong, but she took him out with a single tackle. Just flattened him."

"You got lucky. He would have ripped you to pieces. I can't believe Claire-Marie hung on for so long. You were smart not to move."

"Don't feel so smart right now."

I chuckled. But I didn't feel like laughing. My stomach heaved. I just breathed through it. God, two seconds later and they would have both been dead. If not for Luciana....

Toughen it up sensory immersion chick. Toughen it up.

I tossed the cloth across the room and pulled out a second one. I felt like one of those art restoration people. Except the masterpiece I was revealing wouldn't be all better with a couple of dabs of paint. Ernesto had done a number to his head before Claire-Marie showed up. I raised an eyebrow as the side of the wound became visible. I stole a glance over at Ben, but he wasn't with me. He was somewhere across the city with a little blonde girl whose eyes had gone black. I watched his hands shake.

I looked away.

I hadn't wanted them to know. I hadn't wanted their minds tainted with any of this. I hadn't wanted them to understand...what they were leaving me trapped with.

Goddamn it!

I pressed the back of my wrist to my forehead, trying to push it all back inside. Force it to stay there for just a minute longer.

All this and not one answer. All this for nothing!

Careful not to touch his skin, I lifted Ryan's hair to dab at the rest of the gash. It didn't look like I would need to test my skills with Dr. Hagebak's suture kit. It was more intense road rash than a cut, but the chance that it was infected? If that bubbly section just past his hairline was any indication, pretty freaking high. Couple that with the fact I could feel his body heat vividly through the bath wipe and I suspected a real doctor was in order. Right now.

I dug into the pack and found bandages and antiseptic. I even found a package of antibiotic poppers.

"Is she going to be okay?"

I snapped upright. From the look on his face, Ben had only partially returned from Anna and Matteo's little hideaway.

"What happened to her, Alyse? What happened to all of them?"

I lowered my head for a moment, pressed one of the poppers into Ryan's arm as I took a minute to think.

"I'm not sure exactly. Everybody talks about this Hadria chick, how she does that to them, makes them go crazy. I'm not really sure what that means." I laid a hand on Ben's knee. "But Ben, Anna should be okay. She seems to handle it better than Matteo. She's pretty tough."

Ben just nodded.

I handed him the antiseptic and the pouch of bandages.

"Here, I need you to dress Ryan's little beauty mark."

Ryan cracked the slightest smile. God, he was weak!

Ben finally animated.

"Yeah, yeah, I can do that."

He took my place.

I got up and walked out of the room.

త

I lost it.

My knees came out from under me and I hit the soft grey floorboard on my hands and knees. I rocked with sobs that wracked me so hard my stomach heaved clear to my throat.

"Oh, God!"

I'd left him there, unconscious on the floor, all those soulless ferals screaming at the moon everywhere around the building. And I'd left him there. And now Ryan. How could I protect him if he couldn't even move?

And night was falling.

Night.

I dropped back onto my knees and pressed my face into my hands.

I had only a couple of hours to get them out of here. I smashed my own messed up laugh with my palms.

At least I wouldn't have to use a two-by-four.

God.

You have a call from Tamsin.

Not now, Mo.

The only trick would be getting Ryan down to the water. He was short, but he was solid muscle. A small pack and the raft, fine. But Ryan on those shifting rooftops?

You have another call from Tamsin.

I said, not now, Mo!

She says to tell you to answer no matter what you are doing right now.

My heart thumped suddenly, violently in my chest. I dropped against the wall and wiped madly at my tears.

Audio only.

Alyse? 'Lyse, honey? Oh, just audio. 'Kay. Look, I found something. Not sure exactly what this all means, but there are two squirrelly things here: So, I'm not a doctor, so I don't know exactly what this says about your seizures, but I'm pretty sure Dr. Keith had a copy of your real genetic sequence on file. It wasn't labeled and it was absolutely buried in that mess of files, but it's you with a few adjustments. And the changes...well, they're marked."

"Marked." I stared at the sagging ceiling and stared down the line of mildew. What the hell? "How old's the file? Does it say?"

"Well, some of these files update their date stamps, but it looks like around the time you signed on for the AI surgery."

"And the other thing?"

"Your mom."

"Yeah?"

"Right after you signed on for that surgery, your mom's on the log for a really pricey cancer treatment."

"What?" I sat up and clutched my knees to me.

"Yeah, that's what I said. So I kinda asked her."

"What exactly did you ask her, Tamsin?" My voice held more of a warning than I meant it to.

"I asked if any kind of cancer ran in the family."

"You know it does." She knew about Grandma Anala and Grandpa Don. What the hell kind of question was that?

"Yeah, so I asked her if, you know, she'd had to deal with it at all yet."

"And?"

"She said no."

I blinked. I lowered my gaze from the ceiling to the shredded floral wallpaper across me. I blinked again. A payoff, a bribe.

"Sooo," Tamsin started uncertainly, "you've probably been packing a false DNA tag this whole time, honey."

"And my mother knew."

"Yeah."

"But the—" I cut myself off before I could say 'patch.' I need to remember my own warnings to Ryan about communications. "Nobody knows anything here about any other *adjustments* specifically regarding the seizures."

"Now, I didn't find anything about that here, either. And I really went through those files—every single record, every single thrilling transaction your mechanic ever ran. Sorry it took so long."

"No, we just finished on our side, too. Thanks, Tamsin." The roof's shadow now covered the entire window at the far end of the hall. "I've got to get back now. The boys are waiting for me."

"Alrighty."

We signed off, but I didn't move.

A falsified dog tag. And my mom knew. What could that possibly mean?

Most often falsified DNA IDs are used to mask criminal activity.

Thanks so much for the tip, Mo.

You're welcome.

But that left the million dollar question: Who was hiding behind my fake dog tag? Me? Or one of my parents?

∾

Ben turned from the window when I walked in. We looked at each other, then down to Ryan. Our teammate did not stir at the creak of the boards.

"I got him to eat a little before he fell asleep. Gave him something for the fever—Tamsin gave me her med kit before she left."

I nodded.

"You can't stay," I told Ben without looking up.

"I know."

"I don't know how much longer I have until I turn into one of those things. I'm getting you out of here tonight. He's going to have to get Booth to crack the curtain again." I raised my head and stared my friend ruthlessly in the eye. "Do you think you can get him to do that?"

Ben was the first to look away.

"Yeah."

I crossed the room as quietly as I could and went into what was effectively our "spare bedroom" to start packing. I grabbed the raft and put it next to the window, scanned the room for a daypack. They were all in the other room. I turned back and met Ben in the doorway.

"Why would they plan to open the city if they knew shit like this could happen?"

I flashed back through the last couple of days.

The Asian businessman: *You destroyed everything! Our freedom! My freedom! Years, I fought her for years!*

Jürgen: *So long she has slept. She sleeps no more. Come to me, Alyse. Come to me and live.*

Matteo: *She shouldn't be able to reach us here. How can she reach us here?! Hadria, she's awake. She's too strong. Get out, Alyse! You have to get out!*

"They thought they were safe. They thought they were safe from this Hadria. Something about me being here.... I don't know." I shook my head to clear it from the noise those memories brought with them, chittering in my ears.

"You being here started all this?"

"That's what everyone keeps saying."

Probably because my parents are ex-mafia who had to buy off Dr. Keith to keep our identities secret. Psycho mind-controlling whack jobs always felt threatened by the kid of a Mafioso.

Good, god, what did any of it have to do with anything?!

Nothing.

Not until Ben and Ryan were safe out on the water.

The ferals were terrified of the water.

"The sun is going down." I saw the fear flash in his beautiful brown eyes as they shot to the left to check out the window. He smoothed it over before he looked back down at me. "I've got to finish packing what you'll need. I can't get down to the water until the sun goes down. Jürgen would be on our asses faster that you could dream of paddling. But when I do go, you wake him up and get him to call Booth."

Ben didn't answer. He stared down at me, one hand safely cupped the side of my head over my hair. He pulled me into an awkward embrace, keeping my skin carefully protected from his. With the pressure of his lips against my head, my eyes closed. For a moment, I let down my guard and held onto him, my constant companion for these many years. But then I felt the emotions sliding forward, toward my face. I pulled back before it could shatter my composure.

"I've got to get a pack."

"Yeah, sure. You should keep most of this."

I nodded and moved through the space he made in the doorway. My body moved on autopilot, emptying Ryan's daypack and digging through our baggage in both rooms for food, warmth, and communications.

I came to a halt when I hit a packet of the travel minerals that Dr. Keith had sent with me. The ferals would hunt again tonight. Some base part of me knew this. I looked down at my fancy tattered clothes. The shoes I would keep, but the rest.... From my pile of crap in the corner, I jerked free a pair of cargoes, a fresh winter weave, and some underwear. With my eyes unwaveringly trained on the darkening rooftop, I did a cursory wipe down with a bath wipe.

Falsified dog tag. And my mom knew.

I just couldn't get that out of my head.

I stopped in the middle of hopping into my cargoes.

Should I call and confront her? One call and all these questions could be over? I pictured her vacant, grief stricken face. God. And if she paid off Dr. Keith and never told me, what were the chances she would unload on me now?

It was getting too dark. I jerked the pants the rest of the way on and slipped the sealed mineral packet along with one of those goddamn peanut butter-flavored energy bars into the button pocket on my thigh. I crammed my feet back into the boots and gave my muscles a quick stretch.

It was time to go.

I shouldered the light pack and tucked the raft under one arm. With a nod to Ben, I spun my way out the window.

Mo, call my mom.

Chapter 22

In the call of the moonlight, I balanced on a rooftop above the toxic Adriatic when my mom came online. Red splotches stained her porcelain face and she couldn't catch her breath between sobs to answer my tentative hello.

"Could—could I call you back another time? I'm sorry. It's just a bad moment. I'm so sorry."

"Mom, it's okay."

She signed off before I could say more. Stupid idea. Stupid.

Answers. Please, just one would do! I couldn't stand this anymore!

I turned my face up to that moon draped in stray veils of storm clouds. I could feel that pull; I could feel it draw up my emotions—all of them at once: the joy, the sorrow, the frustration, the anger. I threw my long hair forward to shade my face as if that would somehow protect me.

They would rise soon.

I hurried onward.

I had been down to the water from here, but it had been a flight of grief and self-pity. In the shadows cast by the moon, I couldn't see where the old church's roof held and where it had collapsed. I hunkered down against the rise of the roof and tied the drawstring of the raft to my backpack. I was going to need my hands.

Mo, do you have an image overlay for this rooftop from when we were here last?

Yes.

Pull it up, please.

A transparent picture of the rooftop filled in the shadows before me. I began moving forward on all fours, testing sections as I went.

Which way to the water, Mo?

Forward.

I cleared the top of the church and began to descend. Here was the reason to change to work pants. Two cautious steps, three, four. Bam. Down I went. Sliding down the roof tiles on my ass, the raft beating at me as I went. I dug in my heels, grabbed after a hand-hold. Nothing. Mo's picture promised an end to this ride; the shadows promised a bottomless drop into darkness. One of the tiles broke free and clattered along beside me, rattling like horseshoes over cobblestone.

I hit the adjoining roof.

I took a second to breathe.

Mo, try Uncle Keats.

Just one answer, I begged the string of electrons heading toward California. If anyone still alive would know, it would be my dad's little brother. Just tell me: why was I a lie and why did I have to die for it!

You've reached Keats & Byron Demolition, your number one source—

Shut it off!

Goddamn, where was he? Tahiti?

But I knew where I was now. And I remembered how beaten down this building was, too. I was going to fucking drown before I could find someplace to secure the raft. I must have been unhinged to be wandering around out here.

The building bent to the sea's will about halfway down. I found a section of roof I'd used before, one that dipped down a floor's length to a jumble of rubble that met the sea. Now that I was here, I realized this might not be the best place to launch an inflatable raft. I had no way to tell how shallow this building's watery grave might truly be.

"Shit."

I stripped off the pack and its trailing raft and wedged it into the corner where the fallen roof met a partial wall. As I used both hands to rip off part of the windowsill, my arm remembered my shark god's grip as he rescued me from a fall into this same grave.

But I wasn't half-suicidal right now. I definitely had the give-a-shit to keep myself alive. I had my boys to protect right now. I stepped out into the rubble and began to poke at the water with my stick.

A light flashed.

The rubble, so steady under my cautious feet, rolled and shifted as I scrambled for the partial wall. I just made it around the stonework before the entire building flooded with light.

A searchlight.

These were no ferals. Jürgen. It had to be Jürgen. Apparently, he'd given up on me coming willingly.

The light swept slowly back and forth. I could hear vague voices from the boat. They were not going away. I leaned my head back against the wall and tried to relax.

Why was I a lie?

Maybe not a lie? Maybe a dangerous secret?

I remembered a story about a girl who remained silent for seven years in order to save her brothers from a curse. Her baby was murdered; she was cast out of her kingdom; she became the captive of murderers. Even through all this she remained silent, steadfast. When at last she was to be executed for treason against her own kingdom, the day she was to be strung up on the gallows, the curse broke. Free, her brothers appeared before the king and revealed the reason for her silence. The king restored her to her throne and those who conspired against her hung in her stead.

Why have you stayed silent all these years, Mom? Whose curse have you been hoping time would break?

Now that I was still, I heard the quiet motor. And I heard it shift. The boat and its light began to drift onward.

I began to breathe again.

When the sounds of the motor thinned beyond my hearing, I crept out from behind my wall. With the tip of my stick, I began to map a way out of this mad labyrinth of a city.

Chapter 23

Too much time had passed.

I heard distant predatory screams. Even expecting them, they drove a shudder down the arms that held my balance as I eased over the Gesuiti's rooftop. I prayed Ryan had regained enough strength to make the treacherous journey to the water. Those cries wouldn't stay distant.

I lowered myself toward the barracks/monastery. I froze. That shadow had moved. I stared, willing my night vision to sharpen. There. It moved again.

Aw, shit.

I pulled myself back up on the Gesuiti. I listened. No sounds of violence. No sounds at all. Was I too late or had they not yet attacked?

Mo, ask Ryan if he's alright. Tell him I'm going to draw off the carriers and give him the path to the raft.

Acknowledged.

I released stealth, disposed caution. I would give my boys time to get to the raft. Luciana didn't know, wouldn't understand, but we immersion artists, we already rode with the mad moon.

"Hey, jackasses! I'm right here, ya dumb shits!"

I bolted.

That mad moon flowed like quicksilver in my veins. I was my wolf running through the mist. Mine were the long muscles, the ruffling fur. Mine were the eyes that mirrored souls with the moon's light. I sailed across tiles, barely landing before the next weightless bound. I twisted at the end of the church and rode the slope easily down to the battered ruins below.

I leaped.

I landed on all fours on an uncapped stone wall. My shadows followed.

Across the tops of the labyrinth hedges I flew. Sharp corners, soft brick, I followed those precise lines to where order collapsed into chaos. Mounds of damp debris were my shale hillside. The aged grace of a palatial window beckoned.

I sprang.

With absolute focus, I balanced my body and heaved. My adrenaline boosted me into the open window, its glass pane not even a memory. I perched there, balanced on my toes, looked back at the pack which chased me. They, too, paused. Their leader, a slender woman, long and elegant, unfamiliar, tossed her head at my defiance. Her outrage rose slowly, low in the throat like a big cat's warning growl, growing, building from a snarl to a scream, breaking off in the two-toned shriek of a hawk.

I just smiled.

And slipped into the shadows.

As I'd learned, I kept to the edge of the room, moving lightly from one ghost-filled abode to the next. The building was narrow. Out the next window I found a brace between the two buildings. A bridge for me.

Breaks in the stucco provided temperamental handholds as I scaled my way to the top. I raised my torso onto the brace, pressed myself to standing. I flailed; the brace dropped a centimeter. I ran. I threw myself through the second window as the brace fell to the sea.

One more building. Then two.

The pack drew close now.

I had minutes before they dragged me down.

Two rooftops to choose from, one whole, the other ragged with collapses.

Now to test the levels of their madness.

I ran and sprang. The edge of the stonework caught me in the stomach; the edge of a collapse caught my grip. I ascended.

Each footstep loosed a tile. Every determined grasp widened a collapse. The feral pack climbed mere meters behind me. I heard someone scream. Then a splash. I pushed onward.

Something brushed my ankle. I cocked my leg and kicked. I heard a tumble of tile, a snarl. Then the barest sway began beneath my hands and knees. I straightened and looked back. Behind me two ferals froze. The sway gained in power. The ferals scrambled backward; I scrambled forward.

We all fell.

I grasped the unraveling edge of the roof. Far below perched a stone balcony. Far below. I rolled.

And prayed it would hold.

᠙

The moon rode higher in the night when I woke and came to understand that the balcony had held. I had not. With the adrenaline-spiked madness drained away, I understood with utter clarity how completely I had fucked myself.

There were no signs of the feral carriers. There were, however, absolutely undeniable signs of a broken ankle, possibly a broken rib, and fractured left radius to match the right one so recently healed. I stared down at my beaten body, recognizing these signs, but not registering them. I waited.

My mind remained blank, but my body did not disappoint. The shaking began; both the cold and the shock introduced the pain to me with violence.

While I still could, I reached with my good hand into that pocket where I had stashed the energy bar and the minerals. One set of poppers, one set of pills. Only this time, I wasn't sure it would be enough.

I wedged the packet in between two chunks of tile and tore at it and tore at it and tore at it. Oh, God! I couldn't get it open! I stopped, forced myself to breathe through the panic. I tried again. A piece of the flap tore away. Oh, God! It hurt. It hurt. It hurt!

Stop it!

One more try. A tiny hole. There. Slow down. I snaked a finger inside. Very, very gingerly I widened the tear. The poppers first. I slapped the first one against my jugular. After a futile struggle with my sleeve, the second one went there as well.

I tore the energy bar open with my teeth and stared it down. I knew I was in bad enough shape I might not be able to keep it down. And if I couldn't keep it down, I wouldn't be able to keep the pills down either.

One deep breath, then another.

Breathe out through your toes.

God, not that one!

Breathe.

Bite.

Keep breathing.

No, no, no!

I rolled to my side and puked over the side of the balcony, cracking my forehead against the stone baluster. Tears streamed down my face as my ribs tried to tear themselves apart. Finally, it was done. I rolled back onto my back and stared up at the narrow swatch of sky.

Mo?

Yes.

Margie...Margie...enough to start?

Yes.

Start...my ribs.

The shaking and the pain it inspired consumed my attention as I closed my eyes and waited. Ben. Ryan. Did I give them enough time? Dimly, I recognized Margie prickling to life, her little soldiers issuing forth. Cold. Too cold. The streaks of tears on my face cut like bladed shards of ice.

Mo.

Yes.

Ryan...message.

I bit down on my lips as the tiny demons inside me realigned a shard of bone with a shattered rib. I shouldn't be conscious for this. I shouldn't have to be conscious for this. A doctor wouldn't make me be conscious for this.

A jarring image consumed my brain: my father's one beautiful blue eye, staring. Half of his face absent like a bad computer graphic, exposed bone and flesh hidden away from view by flesh-toned sealant. His satin blonde hair, combed neatly by the nurses, framed that rigid stare. That stare.

Like Grandma Anala.

Like Grandpa Don.

I squeezed my own eyes tight shut.

No, not me, not now.

Not Ryan. Not Ben.

Message Ryan: Are you alright?

Acknowledged.

I stared at the energy bar still clutched in my hand. I knew those poppers weren't enough. This thing had to get down my throat.

I couldn't even force myself to raise it to my lips.

ॐ

The world jerked beneath me, jerked me awake.

The rubble beneath my back shifted.

The balcony.

Instantly, I grabbed after my minerals and my energy bar and clutched them to my chest. I lay perfectly still, chunks of marble and mortar digging fresh divots in my back.

Mo, how far is Margie with the repairs?

Ribs eighty percent complete.

Just the ribs?!

Per the protocol you requested, repairs were halted when the mineral supply was depleted to natural levels.

Cautiously, I shifted my arm to raise the energy bar to my lips. I bit and chewed. But I'd gotten this far before. I relaxed every muscle associated with my stomach and pretended I couldn't feel how this gentling left my battered body vulnerable to even deeper jabs and cuts.

So far so good.

Slow and steady, I reduced the sticky bar by half.

Just a few more bites. Then I could risk those precious pills.

I lifted the bar to my mouth.

I rolled to my side and puked it all into the canal.

Shit! Shit! Shit!

The balcony jerked.

My entire body still heaving, I clamped the pill packet between my teeth and clawed after the windowsill. I got on top of it. With my good foot, I stretched into the darkness for some kind of support beyond it. My toe bumped something. The balcony shrieked, stone against stone. Frantically, I kicked out. A tiny edge of rotten wood.

That would never hold me.

The balcony dropped.

I rolled.

Like a shipwreck survivor, I clung to the inside of the windowsill as the balcony crumbled away. I heard splashes in the water below as chunks of the windowsill came loose in my grip. Stone tumbled free. Lower. Lower. My butt hit the rotten wood. The wood bent. More rock and powdered brick pulverized in my grasp. Was the whole wall coming down?

Then it stopped.

I held perfectly still. Waiting.

Then cautiously, ever so cautiously, centimeter by excruciating centimeter, I scooted my broken body back up on top of the jagged ledge that remained. I pulled the vitamin packet from my teeth and just dangled there, trying to catch my breath, trying to ignore the coating of acid in my mouth.

The energy bar was gone. Not that it mattered.

Ryan and Ben.

Ryan.

He had never called back. Please let him just be asleep! Asleep and then he would wake up and I would be gone, but he would have that message. And he would take Ben to the raft. And they were already gone.

But he would have messaged me back.

And he hadn't.

"Goddamn it!"

Tears of frustration, tears of rage ran fresh streaks down the track on my face.

My arm stung as I raised my hand to clear them away. The sting turned to real pain. I clenched my fist as my position fed too much blood into a huge scrape down my forearm. The dark had weakened and I could see the swath of blood exposed by my torn sleeve.

I stared as the blood began to well in earnest. I knew I should try to turn over, that I should try to elevate it, that I should try...

Mo, would it work?

I kept the image vivid in my mind, vitamins pressed deep into the cut, slowly dissolving as Margie's little bots harvested what they needed.

Yes. But at a significantly decelerated rate.

Decelerated is better than going headfirst into that canal. Better than sitting here waiting to die. Better than never knowing for sure if my boys made it out.

I pushed up on my fractured tibia, not bothering to smother my cry as I twisted those partially healed ribs to get onto my butt. For the longest minute I could only grasp after my leg as the grind of bone sent shudders through me.

Let go.

Let go and start now or this will not change.

Slowly, I pulled my hands away; slowly, I lowered my leg to the irregular rock. I spilled the packet into my shaking palm. My stomach heaved at the mere sight of those pills. Patiently, I breathed through.

Or this will not change.

I turned my bloody arm over and ground the pill deep against rent flesh.

Mo, let's get this party started.

൭

Twice Margie had had to reopen the wound, but as the light found its way down to my narrow shaft of reality, the pills vanished. My ankle had regained full function; I could move my ribs again. Margie couldn't finish my forearm, but I could use it. And that would be enough.

I shifted to my feet, turned my face to that sunlight, and climbed.

Chapter 24

The room was empty.

Not even our packs remained. Splintered floorboards speared the air in memory of a violence my mind recreated all too well.

Gone.

I'd known I would find this. I'd known because I'd found the remains of the raft, shredded and fluttering in the moss on the rubble at the edge of the dark, dark water. I'd known, but still I stood and stared at the rent emptiness.

Slowly, I slid down the wall until I sat, knees tucked up against me. I knew I should not stay here, that this would be the first place they looked when they didn't find my body. But I had nothing left. Nothing left at all.

This is where we had sat—Ryan here next to me, Ben grumbling just a little further on. This is where we had sat, thinking we were so clever, thinking we would unravel the conspiracy of my existence, the decade-old enigma of Sleepers Syndrome through sheer force of will. We had the technology. We had the connections. We had the fresh perspective, the critical new data of me. We thought we were so clever.

And I'd let myself believe it.

So I'd let them stay.

My boys, my boys, my boys!

I didn't want to know this. If I wasn't here, I couldn't know this. I let myself slide the rest of the way to the floor. I curled up on my side, curled up into oblivion.

§

"Alyse, would you make this so easy for me?"

I knew that voice. It brushed my cheek with the fresh sea air. A gentle touch drew my hair back from my face. With a quiet sigh, I rolled toward that voice. The mattress cradled me and the sheet slid and settled over my skin like a fine morning mist, so soothing.

I knew that voice. Always that voice in my dreams.

I opened my eyes. That face looked back at me, regal lines, so beautiful in the light and yet terrifying in its shadows. So near.

With just the tips of his fingers, Jürgen Phan Mai redrew the shape of my naked arm from the shoulder to the bend of the elbow, down to where the hand lay over my belly. I shivered, not just my body, but somewhere deeper, more original. He flattened his hand over mine. Watching me, watching my slightest reaction, he used his open palm to trace his way back up, deliberately brushing the side of my breast beneath the thin sheet. He took my shoulder in a firm grip.

"Would you make this so easy?"

My mouth was open. It wouldn't speak.

I shook my head. Even in dreams, the tears escaped.

"What do you want, Jürgen?" I finally whispered. "What more can you possibly want?"

Shadows swirled through the dark prince's eyes, something fractured and powerful and dangerous and breathtaking in its perfection. This time it was I who watched unrelentingly. This time it was I who pressed forward, rising so easily from the bed, sheet clutched to my breasts. This time it was I who put a hand to his face. I knew this. I knew this.

At my touch, his retreat faltered. We hesitated.

"What...do you want?" I demanded.

The swirl of sheets around me became a swirl of air as the dream collapsed into a spin of despair and yearning. That face vanished beneath my hand, lost in the eddies of mist that glided over me, around me, through me.

"Alyse...."

"Jürgen, answer me. What do you want?"

"I want...I want my boys back."

Furious, I twisted, but he was everywhere and nowhere, his grief, his despair, his longing, craving.

"Goddamn it, Jürgen! They were all I had left! Goddamn you, you son of a bitch!" I clawed at the air, at the nothingness, my hair whipping around me. I nearly didn't hear the whisper through my screams:

"Alyse, they are safe. I kept them safe...for you."

Chapter 25

I opened my eyes. Only a frame of light remained, laying slant across the floor. It illuminated a broken floorboard, a scrap of orange sleeping bag fabric curling up from its splintered tip.

My stomach cramped now that it had an audience. The dry, sticky taste in my mouth was unbearable. I stared at the threads spiraling up from that small swatch of fabric.

My boys.

Jürgen's boys, asleep in a Children's Castle these last ten years. His pain lingered in my chest. Human pain in a man who was nearly no longer human.

He'd saved my boys. Somehow.

But he wouldn't give them back for free. The currency of indebtedness.

I sat up. Something tipped over when I drew my feet forward. I looked to my side. A water bottle and a packet of yogurt. My sprite. Should I cry for the kindness of a woman so mentally broken she didn't recognize the power of her own stench? A woman so bent she cried out at the attack of a space heater and warned of the *fate,* the witch-fairies come to steal my soul?

Yes, I would.

I cracked the water bottle and slowly, carefully cleared my mouth. But my caution was unwarranted. My stomach happily accepted both the water and the food, the cramps gradually easing.

I tipped my head back against the wall. My boys and I had sat here. We'd tried databases and photographs, financial and medical analysis. We found nothing. For ten years now, Jürgen and Dr. Franco had strained their minds and their computers. They found nothing.

I pushed to my feet. I crossed to that broken bit of flooring, pulled the scrap of fabric free. For a moment I ran it across my fingers, then I slipped it into my pocket to take the place of Cirena's sachet that lay somewhere at the bottom of the lagoon. I crossed to the second room, vaulted myself through the window.

My feet and my hands carried me across the church rooftop and then on further to the remains of the raft at the water's edge. I stood with one shoulder propped against the section of wall which had hidden me from the search boat. There, I toyed with that small bit of satiny fabric as I watched the sun sink behind the broken roofs of Father Mauro's island of the dead, Father Mauro who had stolen from the devil's dreams.

Venice, this place, it did not follow the rules of our technology; it did not provide tidy algorithms with tidy outcomes. It played in memory and legend and dream. If I wanted the leverage to free my friends, I would need to play in that same world.

I would need to make a deal with the devil.

&

The last of the day had faded from the thickening clouds when she stepped free of the shadows. I did not turn as she formed herself, but I saw nonetheless. I saw her gather the flickers of starlight, the muted shimmer of the moon and weave them with the dance of the wind. I saw her become.

Technology had told me one true thing: No Cirena existed in the quarantine camp roster of Venice.

But I'd known this.

Just as I'd known she would come.

That tinkling laugh floated on the sea breeze, wrapped my skin in the flush of primal fear. If I'd had nothing to lose, she might have won. But I did. I had so much to lose.

I turned to face her.

She smiled. Her dress of moonlight danced around her to the music of her laughter as she floated toward me. I didn't flinch as she reached out to toy with my dirt and blood crusted hair.

"You finally understand then, little one? So quickly, too. And what will you do with this knowledge, I wonder? Cower with the others behind their foolish protections? Sing to the moon as Hadria rides the night? Give your mind to the madness?

"I will collect my boon." My boon for saving her Anna.

Cirena cocked her head in surprise. Then she clapped her hands with delight.

"So bold! Ah, this will be fun! And what will you wish for, young one?"

"I want to know how it was done. I want to know how this was done to me."

I want to stop it from ever happening again. I want this to be over. Whatever Jürgen demands from me in exchange for those boys, once I secure their freedom, I want this to be over.

I stared her down. Cirena dropped her hands. Slowly, she began circling me, but I twisted to circle with her. She stopped, her back to the sea and the gathering storm. The whip of her silvery hair matched the light of pent up thunder in those seething clouds.

"How it was done?" Her voice no longer carried that lethal note of play. It filled the night like the electric lick of the storm. This was the moment of binding. "How it was done. That is all? Not riches or fine gowns? Not armies to command from a golden throne? Not freedom from this cursed prison? Just to know how it was done?"

A deal with the devil. I would pay for this knowledge in ways I could not yet imagine. Cold flashed through my chest and my heart jerked with a thrill of terror. I straightened. I stepped toward her, my face hard and unrelenting.

"Yes."

"I could give you power over storm and shadow. I could give you lovers to lie at your feet. How it was done? This, I tell you, you do not want, young one."

"And yet, I will have it."

In the midst of her raging storm, Cirena was stillness.

"Very well."

The sky cracked hard enough to shake the rock beneath our feet, but I alone had to regain my footing. Cirena reached out, placed an icy, electric palm on my forehead.

"Alyse Kate Bryant of Kalispell, Montana, your boon is granted."

My body went lax. For a brief flash I saw myself falling toward her. Then I saw nothing. But a whisper chased me into that darkness, a press of lips against my ear:

"Foolish, foolish girl."

Chapter 26

Trees. I was surrounded by trees and grasses and flowers and bushes and moss and lichen. All that life and light surged through me and I drank in the pungent scent of it: the moist mineral-rich earth, the sweet, herbal smell of trampled grass, the deeper, damper scent of the moss at the base of the trees.

Trees. That green light danced over my skin, seeped into my veins, saturating me with clean, beautiful life. The river that sustained them shushed in my ears, soothing that bone-deep fear and worry and pain. Shushed it away.

Almost.

You wanted to know how it happened.

Cirena's voice whispered in my head and I turned.

A young woman picked her way along the tumbled rock shore of the river, one hand pressed to her mouth, one hand lifting her long patchwork skirt. Her waist-length hair covered the straps of her beaded tank top in neat plaits. She sobbed. Her anguish pierced my own chest and I pressed a hand against my own sternum.

My baby. They killed my baby. I let them kill my baby.

She'd had an illegal third. A state-terminated pregnancy. Was that it? Was this my mother who'd been told I'd been terminated? Was this the lie?

The woman raised her head just steps from where I stood. I knew she wouldn't see me, that this was only a memory, but still I froze. I studied that face. She looked so familiar, and yet not.

No, this was not my mother.

She stepped toward me, toward my perfect spot under the dappled light of the trees. Quietly, respectfully I moved aside and relinquished to her her place in the picture.

How could a doctor ever think a vacation would fix this? My baby's dead!

The woman sank to the ground, her multi-colored skirt billowing in the grass around her. She pushed back her tears and stared with empty eyes at the river's swirling edge.

A vacation? That was significant. Where were we? I glanced around, but nothing provided any clues. Carefully, I picked my way down to the water's edge, hoping a landmark might be visible from the river.

"I want my baby back."

I straightened.

Behind me the air rustled, shifted, warmed. I whipped my head around just in time to see his beginning. Like Cirena formed of moonlight, this man drew the gold of sun to create his form. The dappled flashes from between the tree's leaves gathered to one another, gathered into shining golden hair and skin and gleaming sky blue eyes and a sad, sad smile.

A shift in her posture and I knew the woman sensed his presence. She twisted to see him, naked, sculpted radiance stepping clear of his trees. Startled, she pushed to rise. From his great height, he leaned down and placed a hand on her shoulder. Like the will had drained from her entire body, she sank back down to the grass.

In my mind, I heard her faint, confused cry of protest as he lowered her the rest of the way to the ground.

"I will return to you your daughter," he promised her.

He drew away her panties and her exposed legs fell open. In a kind of sick fascination, I watched his buttocks flex as he drove himself into her over and over and over, as my father recreated me for my mother. I felt her filling, straining with too bright energy as she looked up at him, her mind twisted in terror and awe and a lax confusion that would not last.

Too much, too much!

I covered my eyes with my arms as his light, his power flared, washing out everything in a blaze of gold. When I lowered my arms, I saw him propped over her spent, unconscious body. He slid himself free and gently, carefully arranged her skirt to protect her modesty.

I shook my head, just kept shaking my head. Both trembling hands went to my mouth. My whole body shook with the horror of what I watched, with the horror that this sunlight god did not understand.

Not only would this woman have to live with the knowledge of what he had done.

But she would have to give me up.

Again.

❧

"Nana bambin, nana bambin,
e dormi dormi più di una contesa;
to mama la regina,
to padre il conte;
to madre la regina dela tera,
to padre il conte dela primavera

Lullaby, little baby, lullaby
and sleep, sleep more than a countess;
for your mother's the queen,
and your father's the count;
your mother, the queen of the earth,
your father, the count of the spring."

My body swayed in a tight grip as the lullaby went on and on, rhythmic words swaying in my ears, in my mind. Hard rain pelted my face. Through a tight squint I looked up. For a moment, just a brief moment I saw the wild figure of Cirena at the water's edge, more storm than human in form. Her lightning eyes flashed toward me.

"This was never for you to know," she whispered with the wind. "This changes everything. For all of us."

Lightning cracked the low-hung sky.

She was gone.

"Nana bambin, Nana bambin,
and sleep, sleep more than a countess;"

I buried my face in Luciana's sodden rags, clutched her boney arm. She rocked me as she crooned. I didn't smell that rank defense; I felt only her thin hand on my back rubbing at my violent tremors as I saw that scene over and over and over. No way to go back and erase it, no way to undo the wicked gift of my creation.

I understood now. I understood how I would pay for the rest of my life for this knowledge.

Because I knew who that woman was.

Because I knew who that man was.

And so now I knew what I was.

There was no conspiracy of terrorists. There was no missing moment from my life to leave me doubting my reality. No twisting of my genetic code.

"your mother the queen,
your father the count;"

Hugging Luciana's knee, I stared at Lucifer's dreams as they danced and writhed over Father Mauro's sunken workshops. Maps for the damned, navigation charts for the stealers of souls. Twisted and torn, but frozen for a second, like a memory that an entire lifetime could be built on. I stared, almost knowing, almost understanding. A flash. Not a map. Not a map, but a glimpse...of something we were never meant to know. The creation. The destruction. All that is, was, and will ever be. That which lies beyond the artifice, beyond our understanding.

"your mother the queen of the earth,
your father the count of the spring."

No, not a count.
A newly wakened king.

Chapter 27

Jürgen lingered at his office window looking out over the flooded square. He knew I watched. He could feel me just as I felt him.

My boys were somewhere inside that palace.

For just a while longer.

My answer hadn't provided leverage, but instead a deadly secret. I had only one thing to bargain for Ben and Ryan's lives with: my own. And then only with the uncertain belief that Jürgen would release them once the deal was done. Which would win, the feral or the prince? Would he keep them to gain control of me? Or would he honor the deal and his humanity and release them?

I would know all too soon.

But before I released this death-grip on the life I'd believed I'd known, I had something I had to do.

The call connected. A woman's face came into view—a face I hadn't seen in decades until last night. Her grey hair still hung in tidy plaits; the beaded tank top had been traded for heavy velvet with intricate embroidery. Her face was instantly alarmed.

"Alyse, is Simone alright?"

"Yes, the aunt who raised me is fine."

"What?"

"Aunt Becca, *Mother*, I know. I know everything."

Alarm slowly melted into shock, then horror, then crumpled into tears.

"Oh, Alyse, oh, baby. I'm so sorry! We couldn't tell you. They would have taken you away from us. Simone and Carlton, they had no children. You were our third. They would have.... I'm so sorry. How...how on earth did you find out?"

I laughed and looked away from her to stare grimly into the shadows, as if daring the messenger to take form.

"Let's just say I ran into some of my father's relatives."

"Your father's...?"

"I'm in Italy, Aunt Becca."

"In...oh god, no."

"Yeah."

Read on for a special preview

THE SHADES OF VENICE: EPISODE THREE

Portrait in Veronese Green

...coming Fall 2014!

My final work. My final masterpiece. My epitaph.

The decision to relinquish myself to fate, the decision to release control of my false life, left my senses wide open to the world, exquisitely free. Sitting cross-legged in a half-room on the remaining wall of a fallen palazzo, I stretched my arms out, tilted my face up to the cloud-filtered evening sun. That golden sparkle danced along my skin. The sea breeze played through the touch of light over my cheeks, across my throat.

A remembrance of the last days of my humanity.

Mo, open the final scene of Russo's Watch.

Mo, my onboard AI, replaced the ancient, rent architecture around me with the bridge of an interplanetary cruiser, so damaged it should no longer support life. Commander Sarah Russo lay slumped over the command console, her helmsman dead at her feet.

This is where I will begin.

As I drag the character over me, I feel the cold and the pain I'd woven into her body, but I edit out the panic pulsing through her chest. I know now that isn't the truth. There is fear, of course, and with Mo's help I lay it in thread-by-thread along the lines of her shoulders, around the outline of her heart and stomach. But it cannot be that simple.

Because in her defeat, she has won.

The terrorist threat which no one believed is locked in a metal embrace with her own ship, drifting toward the inevitable disintegration of a black hole. Intertwined with that fear are the steel of determination and the fire of the fight not yet extinguished.

Then her personal comm comes to life and all that clarity rips away.

Mo and I work in an eerie synchronicity. She offers files almost before I can ask for them. The early days of my relationship back home with Bryce: that bright joy at the sight of him. Now the later days, pairing the panic and darkness of knowing what hid beneath that joy.

Commander Russo raises herself just enough to face the image of him, the captain of the doomed terrorist freighter. I burst agony around her wounds, strain in the muscles nearly no longer hers to control. Those files are simple enough to find.

He reaches for her. I flood the woman with grief—my father's death, like someone trying to rip my soul from my body. I let her eyes burn with it, let the pressure in her chest and throat and face build with it. Then I pulled it back.

"Sarah, you can still let us go."

Anger doesn't erase the grief as it twists through her jaw. She cannot answer him.

But he will know her answer nonetheless.

I harden the muscles around her eyes as she raises a hand I have hollowed out. She stumbles her fingers across the console. I blur uncertainty through her. She cannot feel the console's haptic feedback. She isn't sure it worked.

Then the ship jerks and shudders. The engines fire one last time.

"Sarah."

His face grows sad as he watches her, understands what she has done. All the noise of emotion falls away into a kind of terrible, peaceful stillness inside her: the moment I decided to trade myself for Ryan and Ben's freedom.

The lovers turn to watch the approach of their deaths. She strains against the inexorable pull of the dead star with the little strength she has left. But soon it begins, like Margie, my onboard medic sending out her nanobots: tiny, sharp pricks, but I cluster them at Sarah's nose, her cheekbones, her forehead.

I interrupt her peace with a fleeting sense of loss. My mother, Simone, Aunt Becca who birthed me, Tamsin, Ryan, Ben...and Ryan's Haylee sleeping her eternal sleep in the Children's Castle. I will never see them again.

That cannot change my mind.

Then the tiny pricks grow vicious like unfed nanobots disassembling my body to keep themselves running: that terrifying night at Dr. Hagebak's hideaway. I build the pressure of a scream in her chest: the night when Matteo turned abruptly from my lover to my attacker.

The movie fades to black.

But I was still here.

I rose on the edge of reality, stretched my own body as the day faded as well. From here, as the sun set, I could see the sad beauty of proud Venice, the reds and brown of her labyrinth of roofs and buildings lent a rich depth in the colored light. *La Serenissima,* The Most Serene Republic.

A political lie that had never been more ironic than now.

File sent.

Thank you, Mo.

With a little too much agility, I vaulted myself into the nearest windowsill on the ancient façade. I crouched there and plucked at a clump of seagrass, watching the Ducal Palace, sensing Jürgen lurking within.

And now, Sarah Russo, it was my turn.

Tonya Macalino

is the national award-winning author of urban fantasy thrillers, SPECTRE OF INTENTION and FACES IN THE WATER. A resident of Hillsboro, Oregon, Tonya lives with her husband, children's author Raymond Macalino, and their two wildly imaginative kids. She is an avid collector of folklore and folk history, far too many to fit comfortably within the pages of any given book! When not working on her latest thriller, she enjoys coaching other writers through the **How to Build a Book** workshops at Jacobsen's Books & More. Tonya also acts as Vice President for NIWA, the Northwest Independent Writers Association.

Want to read more of the little folklore gems she unearthed during her research? Have to know when the next episode of THE SHADES OF VENICE is due out? Love free goodies? Subscribe to The Myth Makers e-newsletter at www.tonyamacalino.com! For weekly news and events, you can also drop by and chat with Tonya on Facebook at www.facebook.com/TonyaMacalino or Twitter @TonyaMacalino.